So Travis had done well for himself

Why shouldn't he have earned a reputation as a great fishing guide? The man had been obsessed with the slimy creatures, after all. If he'd put half as much effort into understanding *her,* she wouldn't have fled the fishing camp crying so hard she could barely see to drive away.

The return drive would be different, Kara promised herself. She wasn't a defenseless, brokenhearted girl anymore, but a mature, capable woman. As the Mercedes turned into the five-acre clearing Travis had christened Bass Busters Fishing Camp, she clutched tightly to her righteous courage. A puny shield against the merciless pounding of her heart.

The place hadn't changed at all!

And there, glittering a shade deeper than the cloudless sky, extending as far as the eye could see across the horizon, was a magnificent faceted sapphire reflecting the October sunshine.

Lake Kimberly, her beautiful enemy.

Kara schooled her features into a mask of indifference. If it killed her, she wouldn't reveal the power of this place—or its owner—to hurt her again.

Dear Reader,

Growing up in a home filled with five females, I often observed that my father would say something, then be totally baffled by the predictable feminine reaction. I also spent many happy hours as a tomboy at the ranch he and his brothers enjoyed as a weekend hunting retreat. At some point while sitting around a potbellied stove or acting as a human bird dog, I learned the language of Texas men— which is the same language other men speak, only cockier.

Hence, long before Ph.D. experts wrote books about the subject, I knew that men and women are from different planets when it comes to communicating and interpreting speech. I've explored this fascinating phenomenon to some extent in each of my novels, but never so specifically as in *Talk to Me*. And talk to me Travis and Kara did!

In telling me their story, they confirmed my belief that love alone can't sustain a relationship between a man and a woman. Good communication skills are essential, and acquiring the ability to listen carefully can be even more important than learning to speak openly and from the heart. Oh, and both Kara and Travis stressed (in separate private interviews so as not to hurt the other's feelings) that developing a good sense of humor is a definite plus.

I hope you enjoy Travis and Kara's journey to enlightenment. If the road gets a little bumpy at times, at least (with these two) it's never boring!

Sincerely,

Jan Freed

P.S. I love hearing from readers and invite you to write me at: 1860 FM 359 #206, Richmond, TX, 77469. Or visit my web site at: www.superauthors.com

TALK TO ME
Jan Freed

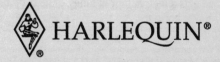

TORONTO • NEW YORK • LONDON
AMSTERDAM • PARIS • SYDNEY • HAMBURG
STOCKHOLM • ATHENS • TOKYO • MILAN • MADRID
PRAGUE • WARSAW • BUDAPEST • AUCKLAND

ISBN 0-373-70858-0

TALK TO ME

To my editor Laura Shin,
who listens carefully to both my writing "voice"
and my author insecurities.

Many thanks for improving my craftsmanship, preventing my
hyperventilation and having a great sense of humor!

CHAPTER ONE

As TOPICS WENT, ''My Significant Other Never Listens To Me'' was about as interesting as a tractor pull. But apparently the rest of Houston had a love life.

Settling into her sixth-row seat, Kara Taylor glanced from the guest chairs and TV cameras on stage to the rapidly filling George R. Brown Convention Center auditorium. Amazing. Hundreds of busy people had wrangled with bosses, baby-sitters and ''five o'clock traffic'' that actually started at three to get here by four. All for a chance to see the touring Los Angeles-based *Vanessa Allen Show*.

Scanning the arriving crowd more closely, Kara arched a brow. Who would've thought so many silk ties and mid-heel pumps would attend the taping?

Oh, she'd known the tabloid talk show was popular. But she'd assumed most fans would be traditional homemakers or senior citizens, like the seventy-three-year-old woman sitting to her right. Gram looked positively giddy at the prospect of seeing her favorite talk-show host in person.

But then, so did the working professionals in the audience—some of whom looked younger than Kara, who'd hit the big three-oh two months ago.

Twisting back around to face the stage, Kara smoothed her navy wool skirt, adjusted her matching jacket, centered the gold heart pendant on her delicate neck chain. Hmph. If she hadn't feared disappointing Gram, who'd raised Kara with unflagging love and selflessness since she was four, no way would she sit here and watch couples air their tawdry dirty laundry. She certainly had better things to do.

Like produce a sleazy lingerie catalog.

Oh God.

Kara battled her flush of chagrin with righteous rationalization. Desperate circumstances called for desperate measures. And *Mystery Woman* merchandise wasn't sleazy. Sexy, yes—to both sexes. At least, it was according to the catalog's photographer, Lisa Williams. Kara would have to continue to trust her best friend's judgment about the fantasies of men.

She would never in a million years comprehend the male psyche.

Women, however, she understood perfectly.

And the delicately feminine, exquisitely detailed lingerie in her catalog would make any woman who wore it feel sexy and beautiful. Results from her first secret experimental mailing had exceeded her wildest hopes. Especially since almost half of the orders had come from men.

If a second city-wide drop pulled the same ten percent response, she wouldn't have to worry about paying double the current rent when Taylor Fine Foundations' lease expired in three months. She wouldn't have to liquidate stock and close the last remaining store in the family's once-thriving chain. She wouldn't have to admit she'd failed to make up for her mother's unforgivable sins.

By the year 2000, she would beat back the wolves from her family's estate and ensure her grandmother's happiness. At least she would if a miracle occurred and those catalogs got mailed out soon.

Yet here she sat in early October, wasting precious hours she couldn't spare, because Gram refused to drive on the freeway, and Major McKinney had bailed from escort duty at the last minute. Wimp. So the retired army officer was running a little fever? He should try running a store with walking pneumonia, the way she had last year, and then complain.

A squeeze on Kara's forearm captured her attention. She glanced down at the hand, as fragile and spotted as a quail's egg, resting on her navy wool sleeve.

"I'm so nervous," Esther Taylor confessed, her pale blue eyes anxious. "Last week a woman in the audience had a big piece of spinach or something in her teeth. It was so embarrassing." She wrinkled her brow. "Do I need more lipstick? Did my hair get mussed in the parking garage?"

Kara's irritation dissolved in an overwhelming rush of affection. Her grandmother was supremely vain.

She checked the vivid pink of Gram's lips, the crisp edges of youth fissured by time and year-round gardening. Her helmet of silver-blue curls hadn't budged, of course. No puny gust of wind could penetrate two coats of Final Net.

"You look wonderful, Gram. Quit worrying."

"You're right. It's not as if Vanessa will pick *me* out of all these people to ask a question on camera. But don't you think this is exciting?"

About as exciting as a bass-fishing tournament. "Hmm-mmm," Kara hummed vaguely, the best she could manage without choking on a lie. Together with a pat on bony knuckles, the sound appeared to satisfy her grandmother.

Just then a frazzled-looking man wearing headphones broke apart from the camera and lighting crew to walk center-stage. He picked up a microphone lying on one chair and tested the sound level, stirring up a buzz of speculation.

"Ladies and gentlemen, could I have your attention, please?" he asked, then repeated the question until the large room quieted. "Ms. Allen will be out shortly. But I'd like to go over a few rules before we start taping.''

Kara then learned she was to stay in her seat at all times, applaud and even laugh on cue, listen carefully to each couple's dialogue on stage without shouting comments—as if she would *do* such a thing—and raise her hand, rise calmly and state her viewpoint succinctly into the microphone if Ms. Allen singled her out of the audience for an opinion.

For the first time since entering the auditorium, Kara experienced a flutter of anxiety. She reached up casually, patted her sleek chignon and tucked a few errant strands into place.

Unnecessary. Vain and silly. She had no intention of raising her hand. Gram was the star-struck fan who'd be thrilled to share the spotlight with her idol.

"All right folks, let's get started," the prompter concluded. "Everybody please give a warm welcome to…*Va-nes-sa Al-len!*''

The familiar theme music swelled. Kara clapped on cue. A tall striking redhead in signature blue-framed glasses entered stage-right carrying a cordless microphone. Her olive-green silk jacket and pants were stylish, but Kara could think of two *Mystery Woman* camisoles that were prettier choices than the one Vanessa wore.

Smiling warmly, the forty-something celebrity waved and shouted, "Howdy, Houston!"

Cheers erupted. Gram warbled a loud, "Howdy!"

"Gosh, I love this city! People here are so friendly. This is my first visit, can you believe that? I thought you'd all have oil wells and, you know, horses and stuff in your backyards, but you don't. You guys have something better." She paused impishly. "Great shopping."

As laughter broke out she grabbed her knees and hitched up both pant cuffs. "Look what I bought today. Ernie, can you get a close-up of these babies?"

Two large screens mounted high on each side of the stage showed the studio audience what the television viewers at home would see. The camera zoomed in on taupe ostrich-skin cowboy boots.

"Aren't they beautiful? Rodeo Drive eat your heart out!" She grinned delightedly.

The crowd roared its approval. Vanessa had acknowledged the city's cosmopolitan status and Texas pride in one fell swoop. No wonder the country loved her. The woman had natural charm and showbiz poise to spare.

Too bad the show's guests often seemed dredged from the bottom of America's barrel of apples. Watching rotten characters unpeeled and exposed on TV was not Kara's idea of entertainment.

Viewing the same process—live and unedited in her naive past—had been bad enough.

"We have some interesting guests for you to-day," Vanessa was saying. "Each of the couples you'll meet is at the brink of breaking up because of a communication problem in their relationship. Let's see if we can help these people out. What do you say, folks?"

Kara squirmed through the audience's enthusi-astic response and Vanessa's introduction of Bill and Dorothy, an overweight, middle-aged couple from Rosenberg, Texas.

The two settled in their chairs, his finger prying more space between red neck and shirt collar, her fists tugging less space between knees and skirt hem. They fidgeted self-consciously while Vanessa headed down the stage steps and into the center aisle. Two men bracing cameras on their shoulders followed, as well as the stage manager who'd opened the show, carrying a second microphone.

Esther squeezed Kara's arm and drew in a sharp breath, then released a disappointed sigh when Vanessa passed by their row.

About halfway up the aisle the TV host stopped and turned.

"Now then, Dorothy, let's start with you. You told our producer that your husband hasn't talked to you in *twenty-seven* years of marriage, and that you can't take it anymore. Do you honestly mean to say he hasn't spoken to you in all that time?"

"Oh, he's spoken, all right. He just hasn't *talked*

to me,'' Dorothy clarified in an unpleasantly shrill voice.

"Can you be more specific?"

"Well, like about a week ago? He comes home from work and I ask him how his day was. 'Okay,' he says, like it was business as usual. So later I'm watching the news, and there's a story about a chemical leak at the plant where he works."

She flicked a resentful glance at her husband, who gazed stonily ahead. "He could've been hurt bad, and I have to find out about it on Channel 2! Does that sound like an 'okay' day to you?"

"Nobody got hurt," Bill spoke up, frowning at the audience. "They cleaned up the spill and I was back on the job in a couple of hours. Like I said, it was an okay day."

Huffing, Dorothy turned in her chair to face him directly. "What about last night during *Walker, Texas Ranger*? I asked if you were nervous about being on the show today, and you never even looked away from the TV."

"I answered you, didn't I?"

"You said 'yeah.' Period. What kind of answer is that? For all I know you didn't even hear me!"

Bill winced and stuck his little finger in one ear. "The whole trailer park heard you, Dorothy. How can you think I didn't?"

Predominantly male laughter swelled in the audience.

Kara bristled.

She knew how Dorothy had thought her husband hadn't heard. He hadn't *looked* at her, that's how. Without the connection of eye contact, a wife simply couldn't be sure her husband was paying attention.

Poor Dorothy's cheeks were tomato red. "If you'd told me how you were feeling, if you'd *talked* to me I would have known you heard me. But all you said was 'yeah.' And then when I told you I was nervous, too, and that my stomach felt queasy every time I thought about being on TV, you got mad."

The couple fumed silently.

Vanessa jumped in fast. "Is that true, Bill?"

His scowl deepened. "I guess."

Kara's indignation on his wife's behalf rose. From the outbreak of feminine murmurs in the crowd, she wasn't alone.

"Why would her sympathy make you mad?" Vanessa sounded sincerely puzzled.

Slouched in his chair, Bill retreated into himself and stared at an exit sign. Rudely silent. Aloofly distant.

Annoyingly familiar.

Kara wanted to rush up on stage and shake an answer out of the man.

"See what I mean?" Dorothy turned away from the husband who hadn't looked at her since they'd entered the stage. "It's hopeless. When he's at the pool hall with his buddies, he yaks his head off. But he won't say squat to me, who's given him three children and cooked and cleaned for him twenty-seven years. I give up."

"No, no," Vanessa protested. "Give the audience a chance to help. Okay folks, who'd like to comment on Bill and Dorothy's problem?"

Hands, including Esther's, shot up everywhere. But Vanessa was plunging into the opposite section of the auditorium.

"Let's get a man's take on this, first. The gentleman with the dark hair, sitting in the middle. Yes, you, I'm heading your way."

Kara twisted and craned along with everyone else to watch Vanessa's progress. Too many heads blocked the view.

"Stand up, sir—whoa! Hello up there. Everything *is* bigger in Texas, isn't it? Love the T-shirt, by the way."

Kara jockeyed for a glimpse of the man. Darn it, she couldn't see!

"Turn toward the camera so we can zoom in for the folks at home. That's it. *Women want me. Bass fear me,*" Vanessa read, her tone amused.

Kara's heart stopped cold...then lurched into heavy slamming beats.

Remembering the big-screen monitor, she whirled to the front. The camera had focused on thin gray cotton stretched tightly over a muscular chest. Dead center, a hooked bass thrashed out of the water, the once-vivid greens and blues faded, the words above imprinted forever in Kara's memory.

"Tell us what your name is, sir, and where you're from."

Even before the camera moved, even before the man answered, Kara knew.

Oh God, oh God.

"My name is Travis Malloy, and I'm from Lake Kimberly, Texas," drawled the deep baritone that had so enthralled a young woman accustomed primarily to feminine voices.

Gram gasped.

The camera pulled back.

Kara stared at the shaggy sable hair, the slightly crooked nose, the square masculine jaw sporting stubble—not for fashion's sake but because his beard grew at the speed of light. She took in the bronzed skin and deep squint lines of an outdoorsman, the dark intelligent eyes of a voracious reader.

Then she assembled it all into the heartbreaker of a face she hadn't seen in nine years. The face of her ex-husband. The man who had, in fact, broken her heart—and had the supreme gall now to wear the T-shirt she'd given him for their first-year anniversary celebration.

The same occasion he'd ended their marriage for good.

STANDING IN THE beam of a remote-camera spotlight, Travis silently cursed the irritation that had sent up his hand, along with seventy or so others.

To his right, obnoxious cackling heated his neck. He probed with his heavy boot until he bumped rubber, then carefully planted his full weight on top of a sneaker.

"Okay, Travis," Vanessa said above Jake's strangled groan. "What did you want to say to Dorothy and Bill?"

Since "never mind" would make an even bigger fool out of him, Travis eased off his little brother's foot and onto the subject at hand. "Just that I think I know why Bill got mad when Dorothy told him she was nervous and queasy."

"Really? Why?"

He'd had nine years to refine his answer.

"Because instead of focusing on him, she brought the conversation right back to her. Why should he 'talk' to her about his feelings when she doesn't respect them enough to devote her full attention to them?"

Vanessa appeared surprised, then intrigued. "Interesting. I see a lot of men in the audience nodding their heads. What about you, Bill?" she said, turning to the stage. "Can you confirm Travis's theory?"

Bill had snapped to military attention, amazed gratitude replacing his earlier scowl. "Yeah. I could never quite put my finger on it before, but that's exactly right. Hey, thanks, buddy."

Travis shrugged modestly. Unlike most women, he could be right without making a federal case out of it.

"I'm impressed, Travis. Thank you," Vanessa told him in a dismissive tone.

He gladly sank out of the spotlight into his seat, ignoring the low singsong, "teacher's pet" from his right. Give Jake an inch of encouragement and he'd dole out a mile of abuse.

Travis couldn't think why he'd accepted tickets to the *Vanessa Allen Show* in lieu of his normal fishing-guide fee. Or why he'd compounded the mistake by inviting the Malloy family clown to accompany him to the show.

"Dorothy, you look a little shocked," Vanessa continued. "What do you think about all this?"

Dorothy closed her sagging jaw. "I can't believe what I'm hearing. Do you really think I don't respect your feelings, Bill?"

"I said so, didn't I?"

"For heaven's sake, *look* at me, please."

Travis cringed, the words fingernails on the blackboard of his memory, a slate he'd yet to wipe clean. He should never have made the rare trip into Houston today.

When Bill finally gazed at his wife, his expression was long-suffering. "All I know is, whenever I tell you something personal, you always say how *you're* feeling or what happened to you that was almost the same. Like what *I* feel isn't important."

"But—Bill, honey, that's not at *all* what I think. When I say those things, I only want you to know you're not alone, that I've felt the same way. I thought that knowing I understand how you feel might comfort you."

"Well, it doesn't. It never has."

"I didn't know." Dorothy's strident voice was subdued, her two screen-monitor faces sincere and misty-eyed. "I swear I didn't know. I…I'm sorry."

Travis shifted uneasily. The conversation slowly faded into the background of his mind. A soft melodious voice crept forward from the past.

Look at me, please.

Talk to me, please.

I know exactly how you feel about not making the boat payment on time. The late fees I paid on rent for my apartment in college would add up to a nice little nest egg. Don't worry about it, Travis.

Had his ex-wife possibly meant to comfort him instead of belittle his real worries about the future?

Uh-uh. No way, José. Did not compute. Nice try, but no bananas.

She'd had no interest at all in helping him establish a fishing camp on the shores of Lake Kimberly. It was as simple as that. They'd been as mismatched as caviar and catfish bait, their marriage doomed from the start.

Of all the females he'd never understood—which at age thirty-four was a hell of a long list—Travis had never understood Kara Taylor the most.

Men, on the other hand, were an open book. As proof, he'd developed Bass Busters Fishing Camp into a thriving operation.

An elbow in his ribs jabbed Travis into the present.

"Man, can you believe this?" Jake muttered, gesturing to the stage. "The Simpsons meet The Munsters."

Travis checked out the teenage couple sitting next to Bill and Dorothy, and felt his lips twitch.

The big brawny dude wore black jeans, a black T-shirt and black biker boots. He had massive shoulders, a low ridged forehead and a flat-top haircut. Put bolts in his neck and he could pass for Herman Munster's little brother. The girl's long black hair, flowing black dress and cadaver-pale face with heavily lined eyes made a fitting match.

Vanessa spoke from the center aisle. "Since we heard from Dorothy first, last time, let's start now with you, Terrence. Tell us why Tiffany doesn't understand you."

Travis and Jake shared an incredulous look.

"Terrence?" Jake mouthed silently.

"Tiffany?" Travis mouthed back.

They both snorted at the incongruous names.

"She's always puttin' me down, man, and then acts all hurt when I say so. Like, the other night at Sonic? They've got this deal where if you don't get your order delivered in fifteen minutes, you get it free?

"So I'm keepin' an eye on my watch, ya know? The waitress skates up with our burgers, and I tell her she's five minutes late. But Tiffany, she says— real loud—that I'm wrong and the food's not late. And everybody's car windows are down for the trays."

Travis winced in sympathy.

"Why doesn't she just scream 'Loser' to my face?" Terrence asked the audience.

"Oh, puh-leez!" Tiffany rolled her eyes, a star-tlingly melodramatic sight given her heavy make-up. "Your watch was fast. Kim wasn't late. She gets in trouble if she gives out too many coupons in a night."

"Whose side are you on? Hers or mine?"

"That's stupid. You're my boyfriend. I'm always on your side."

"Then why did you put me down?"

"I *didn't* put you down. I helped out a friend!"

"See? You're on her side."

Tiffany let out a frustrated shriek, lifted her hands and strangled an invisible neck.

As the women in the audience laughed, Vanessa moved to the section opposite Travis and Jake.

"Who has a comment?" she asked, weaving into the crowd. "Yes, sir, tell us your name and what's on your mind."

A short, balding man stood and thrust out his chin. "Harold Stokes. And I think if she was really on his side, she wouldn't have contradicted him in public."

"Thank you, Harold." Vanessa moved closer to the stage. "The men are all nodding again. Let's get a female point of view. Ah, there's a woman of experience. Hang on, I'm coming. Okay, what's your name?"

The sound of amplified breathing filled the auditorium.

"Don't be shy, dear. We're all friends."

Travis's gaze sought the closest monitor—and widened.

Good grief! He'd recognize that sweet face surrounded by immovable gray curls anywhere.

Esther Taylor stood frozen in the spotlight, prime for gigging or a truck bumper in her gut. She eyed the extended microphone as if it were a hand grenade with the pin pulled.

The audience started to mumble and snicker.

Move on to someone else. Don't prolong the old girl's misery.

Esther sat abruptly, yanked down by an unseen force, and a mint-julep voice spoke. "I'll comment, if you'd like."

Travis's heart sputtered like a flooded outboard motor. Even before the camera moved, he knew.

"Wonderful! Stand up and tell us your name."

Of all the crazy rotten luck.

"Kara Taylor. And the lady who just sat and will kill herself when we get home is your biggest fan— Esther Taylor, my grandmother."

Travis stared at the tall elegant woman who'd disarmed the restless audience as quickly and easily as she'd once entranced him.

Her generous curves were disguised by a severe navy jacket and skirt, her only accessory a dainty necklace. Her glorious platinum-blond hair was tortured into some sort of do only women liked. Her bewitching green eyes were underscored by shadowed half moons of fatigue.

Together they formed the heartbreaking beauty he hadn't seen in nine years. His ex-wife. The woman who had, in fact, broken his heart—and had the incredible gall now to wear the heart pendant he'd given her to celebrate their first-year anniversary.

The same occasion she'd ended their marriage for good.

CHAPTER TWO

KARA WONDERED when the prickles at her hairline would drip tears of sweat for all of America—and Travis—to see. The spotlight was incredibly hot… both literally and figuratively.

"So tell us, Kara, what do you think about Terrence's claim that Tiffany always puts him down?" Vanessa tipped her microphone.

Esther Taylor would expect a ladylike answer. But Kara figured Gram owed her. "Well, I don't know what Tiffany 'always' does. But what she did at Sonic was act in a mature, caring and responsible way that had nothing to do with anyone but the waitress. I think Terrence needs to grow up," Kara said bluntly.

A smattering of applause broke out from some of the women in the audience, along with a few grumbles from the men.

Vanessa perked up at the scent of a lively debate. "Them thar's fightin' words, Kara. Can you define the phrase *grow up?*"

Where to start, that was the harder question. "Let's backtrack to Bill and Dorothy," Kara began.

"He said she doesn't respect his feelings, yet he doesn't supply her with any clues as to what they are. So she prods and probes and shares her own feelings in hopes he'll cough up some of his. Which of course, he doesn't.

"After all, that would be the mature thing to do. Instead, he expects her to read his mind, then pouts like a three-year-old when she isn't psychic."

The spontaneous applause and grumbles were louder than before.

Vanessa held up a quieting hand. "Danny?" She searched the auditorium and located the stage manager. "I want to stay with Kara a minute. Can you work that side of the room for the male point of view?"

He nodded and moved toward the back row.

Vanessa's gaze returned to Kara. "And Terrence? How was his behavior immature?"

Blocking out the camera and her grandmother's distressed gaze, Kara concentrated on the gleam of encouragement in Vanessa's eyes.

"First of all, he seems to think the world revolves around him. As if everyone at Sonic was more interested in what he was doing than in eating their fries. I mean, get real. That's so arrogant, so typically *male*.

"And so what if everyone *did* hear Tiffany correct him about the time?" Kara continued, picking up steam. "I've got a news flash for him. His watch was fast *and he was wrong.* But did he apologize to the waitress? No-o, that would've been the mature thing to do.

"Instead, he got mad at Tiffany and accused her of embarrassing him in public. Because, bottom line, most men don't care if they're actually right or not. The only important thing to them is that other people *think* they are!"

A thunderous wave of applause and feminine cheers buoyed Kara's ego. This was starting to get fun. She glanced at the monitor just as a teen in full rapper gear rose from his seat and lowered his mouth to Danny's microphone.

"A woman shouldn't dis her man, you know what I'm sayin', Mama? An' if she does—" he hitched one shoulder and looked away, then gazed deliberately back into the camera "—he should *dump* her ass! Wha' dya think of that?"

Kara waited for the rumble of male approval to fade, then said, "I think you missed your nap this afternoon."

The audience erupted into laughter, a balanced mix of high and deep tones. Gram reached up and squeezed Kara's hand briefly, whether in approval or caution wasn't clear.

Still smiling, Vanessa shook her head. "I should put you up against that fish guy—what's his name?"

Uh-oh.

"Travis!" Gram trilled.

Great, Kara thought. *Now* she talks.

"Oh, yeah, Travis. Danny, head over his way would you? I'm dying to know what he has to say. You men in the audience want to let him speak for you?" Vanessa cocked her head and cupped an ear. "What's that?"

The men roared yes.

Kara watched the monitor sickly as the camera zoomed in on Travis, who was being prodded and shoved into standing by the man sitting next to him. Good grief, was that grinning replica of her ex-husband really *Jake?*

"Hi, Travis." Vanessa directed a beauty-queen wave across the auditorium. "I want you to meet Kara. Kara, say hello to Travis."

Kara opened her mouth, but nothing came out.

"You'll have to do better than that, girl," Vanessa teased amid the chuckles. "The women here are counting on you. So Travis, do you agree with Kara that Terrence should've apologized to the waitress instead of getting mad at Tiffany?"

"No. Kara always—I mean, from what I've seen, she appears to lose the big picture in favor of petty details. The issue here isn't whether Terrence was right or wrong about the food being late. The issue is respect and loyalty."

That old song and dance?

"I've got a question for Kara," Travis continued.

"Let's pretend the shoe was on the other foot and Terrence had told Tiffany in a real loud voice that…oh, that her hair needed washing, for example. And everybody at Sonic heard. Are you telling me that Tiffany wouldn't get mad at him?"

"That's different and you know it. You're talking about an intimate comment on a person's appearance, whereas I'm referring to a correct or incorrect fact. The waitress was either late, or she wasn't. Nothing personal involved."

"See now, Kara, you weren't listening to me."

Ladies do not scream obscenities or foam at the mouth.

"The larger issue isn't about time or dirty hair," he continued in the condescending tone that had always set her teeth on edge. "It's about having enough respect for the other person that you either lower your voice so the whole city can't hear you, or postpone the conversation until you're alone."

She sniffed. "As I said, what complete strangers think is more important to a man than what his significant other thinks."

"That's so irrational, so typically *female,*" he mimicked, twisting her earlier words to his advantage.

"Oh, really?" Disconcerting, talking to a television monitor. Especially when his image kept dissolving into hers.

Kara turned toward the tall, spotlighted figure

near the back of the auditorium. She didn't need to see his features to sense his every blink. "Then tell me why a man won't stop and ask for directions?"

A beat of silence. "Excuse me?"

"If men don't care more about what a complete stranger thinks than what their significant others think, why will they keep driving in circles when we're tired and hungry and ready to *get there,* instead of stopping to ask a stranger for directions?"

Every woman in the audience chuckled at that one, but Kara barely heard.

All her senses were tuned into the signals crackling above the sea of heads. A confusing, exhilarating, frightening exchange she hadn't experienced in nine years.

He shifted his stance, and the connection broke. "We don't stop and ask complete strangers because they may not know the right directions."

Kara blinked. "You're kidding."

"No. They could give us completely wrong directions and we'd be worse off than before."

"My, God, you *are* serious. If people don't know the directions, Travis, they'll tell you they don't know."

"Not if they're embarrassed to admit they don't know."

"Oh, well, you're talking about male strangers. A woman would never consciously hurt someone just to save face, like Terrance was willing to hurt that waitress because he was embarrassed to admit he was wrong. Thanks for clearing that up.''

''Hey, that's not what I—''

''Whoa-whoa-whoa,'' Vanessa interrupted, laughing into the camera. ''Time out. I created a couple of monsters here. We have to take a commercial break, but don't go away folks. We'll be right back with our next couple and more fascinating debate.''

The remote-camera spotlight cut off.

Kara groped blindly for her seat, hit cotton candy hair and stumbled to the left. She sat with a sigh of relief.

''Boy, you and Travis are something else!'' Vanessa exulted to Kara. ''I'd love to keep the discussion going, but I've gotta move on to other opinions. Maybe I'll get back to you guys later.''

She leaned down and spoke for Kara's ears alone. ''You kicked butt. Fish man didn't stand a chance.''

Remembering the currents leaping between her and Travis, Kara smiled weakly, glad an auditorium had separated them. Proximity to her ex-husband had always scrambled her brains. Whatever quirk of fate had delivered them to the same auditorium today, Kara didn't plan on reading too much into it.

If she didn't bump into him for another nine years, that would be far too soon for her.

Ross Hadley slumped in his auditorium chair, oblivious to the third couple whining on stage.

The flawlessly produced road show, which he'd attended in hopes of picking up pointers, couldn't compete with the tingly sensation in his abdomen. The one signaling something out of the ordinary. The gut-deep feeling he'd rarely experienced but had learned not to ignore.

The last time he'd tingled was three years ago, when Sally had dragged him to "Cooking for Couples" classes on the advice of their counselor. His sharing an activity that was important to her hadn't salvaged their marriage, but it had boosted his reputation at KLUV-TV, Houston. The better result for all concerned.

The instructor that fateful night had been a pretentious British ass named Henry Frey. He clearly hadn't wanted to teach seventeen amateur gourmets any more than one workaholic fast-food junkie had wanted to learn.

Ten minutes into class, Ross had awakened and smelled the Earl Grey tea.

He recognized good broadcast entertainment when he saw it, and Henry had been a natural talent. His monologue on American culture, as cynical as Americans themselves, had been delivered in a snooty British accent that made his sarcasm seem terribly witty. And his flamboyant style of mixing

ingredients and kneading dough added visual interest to the stand-up comedy routine.

As associate producer of *Meet Houston* at the
time, Ross had known the pastry chef would make
an excellent guest. But…there'd been that odd tingle in his gut.

So he'd pitched and sold station management on
launching *The Bantering Baker*—hiring Ross as the
show's full-fledged producer, of course. Then he'd
worked sixteen-hour shifts to achieve network-
program quality on a cheesy local-show budget.
Ratings had slowly climbed, his career moving
right on track…until he'd been derailed.

Sabotaged by rum balls, whiskey sour cake and
Henry's fondness for the key ingredients.

Glowering now, Ross acknowledged that the
show's ratings, and its star, had stumbled once too
often in recent months. *The Bantering Baker* would
be canceled.

Producer openings were scarce, the competition
ruthless, past performance was everything, and his
wouldn't look too hot on a resumé. He'd failed to
"handle" his on-air talent's excesses. As a result,
he could experience a major setback in his career.

Or, he could create another new show.

Ross straightened his spine, thankful he'd chosen
to sit in the back row for the *Vanessa Allen Show*
taping. The nosebleed section of the tiered audito-

rium provided a sweeping overview of the audience.

He easily located Travis Malloy, bold interpreter and defender of men. A guy whom bass feared, women wanted and the camera absolutely loved.

In addition to rugged good looks, he possessed a decent command of language and logic. The spotlight hadn't intimidated him. Nor had Vanessa.

Very very good.

He wasn't introverted or painfully shy. Neither had he come across as a loud belligerent oaf. He'd simply sounded confident he was right. The perfect attitude. At least, ideal for what Ross had in mind.

His gaze moved to the left and down, zeroing in on a bright blond head six rows back from the stage.

Kara Taylor. Unusual first name, but then, that hadn't hurt Ricki Lake. Kara displayed Ricki's same accessible charm, plus a beauty more striking than classical.

If the camera loved Travis, it worshiped Kara's creamy skin, exotic cat's eyes and unusual silver-gold hair.

Ross had underestimated her brain at first. Vapid blondes were rampant in the entertainment industry. Yet he'd quickly seen that in a duel of wits, she was a master verbal fencer. An able champion of women's confusing thought patterns.

The national spotlight hadn't rattled her a bit.

Even better, when she'd faced Travis across the auditorium, vibrant energy had snapped and crackled between them. A fascinating phenomenon to watch. The kind of visible chemistry that was the stuff of every television producer's dreams.

As a concept crystallized in Ross's mind, the tingle in his gut became burning excitement.

His success depended as much on sheer luck as on negotiating skill. But nothing ventured, nothing gained, and he had everything to lose by passively accepting his fate.

Okay. He would do it.

Finalize his game plan and speak to the principle players ASAP, a delicate task. They would ask many questions, introduce unknown obstacles. Not that Ross doubted the two strangers would eventually say yes.

After all, for a shot at fame and fortune, even mortal enemies would agree to join forces.

AT ELEVEN O'CLOCK the next day, phone snugged between ear and shoulder, Kara tuned out Vinnie's New York accent and lined up five newly developed contact sheets. Not for the first time, she wished for an art table. One day, maybe. Right now the back office at Taylor Fine Foundations barely accommodated her battered desk and single guest chair.

Leaning closer, she moved her magnifying loupe

over a row of tiny photographs. The lavender bra and matching silk tap pants shimmered sensuously. Using candlelight had been inspired. If Lisa weren't independently wealthy and easily bored, she could earn a living as a photographer.

Without lifting her gaze, Kara gave a quick thumbs-up.

"Yesss!" her friend exulted.

Kara grinned and adjusted the loupe's frame. They could crop in close but leave the draped blond curl teasing a scalloped lace cup—

"*Kara?*"

She jerked, recaptured the slipping phone and leaned back into imitation leather. "Yes, Vinnie?"

"Did you hear a word I said?"

"Of course I heard," she bluffed.

"Well?"

Fortunately the businessman she'd only dealt with via phone, fax, e-mail and air express was unflaggingly single-minded. His cost-consciousness was one reason why Spinelli Printing offered the highest quality and best value for the dollar.

"Well," Kara responded, "I know you 'cut me a break' on the first catalogs. That's why I'm not bidding this job out to other printers. Take two thousand off the estimate you faxed, and I'll continue to give you first chance at printing all future *Mystery Woman* catalogs."

"Two thousand! You gotta be kiddin', doll—"

"I'm nobody's doll," Kara corrected mildly, "But I'm quite serious about continuing to use Spinelli Printing. 'Dance with the one who brung ya,' that's my motto. Work with me now on lowering your cost, and when the catalog goes national we'll waltz into the big time together." She winked shamelessly at Lisa, who rolled her eyes.

"Nothing personal, babe, but I got alimony and child support up the wazoo. I'm not running a friggin' charity, ya know."

Kara stiffened.

"I got a business to keep afloat."

So did she. And Taylor Fine Foundations was sinking faster than she could bail. Her grandmother would be appalled at what she was about to do. But she'd learned long ago that a "lady" in business became a "sucker" if she didn't play her own version of hardball.

"Speaking of charity, Vinnie...I had nothing to gain in July by referring Township Square's advertising department to Spinelli Printing. Don't misunderstand. I didn't expect a commission—although that wouldn't have been *in*appropriate." She paused delicately. "I *was* surprised not to get a thank-you note, given the value of your new account. My guess is your profits on the Labor Day Sale insert alone paid for at least six months of child support."

From Vinnie's startled silence, she'd guessed right.

"Ka-ra," he finally said in a conciliatory tone. "I feel terrible. Didn't you get the roses I told Susan to send you?"

Unbelievable. He was actually pinning his poor business etiquette on his overworked secretary. "No, I didn't."

"I gotta admit I was a little surprised when you never mentioned them. Now I understand. You'll forgive Susan, won't you?"

The weasel! "I never blamed her in the first place."

"You're terrific, babe. One in a million. And I really do appreciate your referral. Township Square's a nice little account."

Nice little account?

Meeting Lisa's gaze, Kara ignored the sudden alarm in her friend's alert brown eyes. "Gee, Vinnie, that's odd. Susan said you told her Township Square was Spinelli Printing's largest account. And we both know she never forgets a thing you tell her, don't we? Not that I'm going to argue semantics with you, or I'd have to explain why calling me 'babe' and 'doll' is as politically incorrect, unenlightened and offensive as my calling you an obnoxious Yankee with the manners of a—" Kara broke off and glared "—*what?*"

Lisa ceased her frantic slashing motions.

"Pig?" Vinnie supplied in a suspicious tone.

Common sense returned in a rush of chagrin. Kara forced a weak laugh. "You always did have a good sense of humor, Vinnie. Some people flat don't get my jokes. Look, all I'm asking is that you settle for a modest markup on these next catalogs. You won't be sorry. *Mystery Woman* is a winner. You said so yourself."

"I said the model you're using is a winner." A lascivious note had entered his voice. "Now, you get me a date with *her* and I'll knock two grand off my estimate, no problem."

Distaste warred with a stir of interest. "Are you serious?"

"You mean...*you* are? Sweet Mary, Jesus and Joseph! Can you really set me up with the Mystery Woman?"

Caution battled with her knowledge of the company's dwindling bank account. "I didn't say that. I don't know how she feels about blind dates. I can't even tell her what you look like."

"Five eleven, dark hair, brown eyes. A regular Italian stallion. Think Rocky, before he got too skinny."

Wisdom fought with Kara's image of Gram's crushed expression should her beloved husband's family business go bankrupt. "I don't know, Vinnie. I can't see her flying all the way to New Jersey, even if you paid her air fare."

"For a date with the Mystery Woman, I'd fly to Houston in a heartbeat, maybe try and drum up a little more business while I'm there. My kid's with me through the weekend, but the next two weeks are clear. How 'bout giving her a call, Kara?"

The sound of her name snapped Kara into lucidity. She had no business meddling with the Mystery Woman's privacy. "I'm sorry, Vinnie. I won't compromise my working relationship with her *or* you. Besides, her schedule is just so hectic—"

"I'll print your catalogs at cost," he interrupted. "Zero markup. You'll save three, maybe four grand."

Kara blinked.

"C'mon, doll. What d'ya say?"

CHAPTER THREE

GREED WAVED a victory banner Kara couldn't ignore. "I say a girl's gotta eat sometime, right? I'm sure she can squeeze in a dinner date during the next month. Let me call her and get back to you soon."

"Great! Oh, man, a date with the Mystery Woman," he crowed. "Wait'll the guys in the shop hear about this. They drooled so much over the last catalog the ink took twice as long to dry."

Oh God.

"What's her name, by the way?"

Kara pressed cool knuckles against a heated cheek. "The modeling agency is very strict about guarding its clients. If she agrees to meet you, I'll let her tell you herself."

"Well…I guess that's fair."

Thank goodness.

"A hot babe like that must worry about stalkers and stuff."

Oh God.

"You call me as soon as you talk to her, okay, Kara?"

"I'll do that, Vinnie. Bye now."

"See ya, doll."

Carefully replacing the receiver, Kara assumed a casual expression and cleared her throat. "That was Vinnie."

Lisa Williams leveled the lovely brown gaze that made small boys fight to crawl onto her lap and men scramble to pull out her chair. Ebony-haired, porcelain-skinned and five foot three in her highest Bruno Magli heels, she drew protective males with her petite femininity faster than Jane could yodel up Tarzan.

Kara, standing five foot nine inches sans heels, had always felt like an Amazon in comparison—especially in grade school, when she'd also towered above the boys. Small as her best friend was, when it came to Lisa and the opposite sex, Kara knew exactly who wore the loincloth.

She'd be lucky to stave off the impending lecture. "Just hold your comments until I can explain, Lisa."

"Tell me you didn't promise that man a date with the Mystery Woman and I'll be quiet."

"Okay. I didn't promise that man a date wi—"

"Damn it, Kara, would you mind explaining why we've been more secretive than 007 all these months if you don't mind blowing your cover? Are you *crazy*?"

Sighing, Kara glanced at the unpaid vendor invoices stacked in order of squeakiest wheel. "Not yet. But I'm getting there."

Lisa's indignant glare became a worried frown. "You look exhausted. Something's happened you're not telling me. I sensed it even before Vinnie's call. Big trouble?"

Six feet four of it, crowding her dreams last night with hurtful memories and erotic images.

Kara resisted the urge to mention her bizarre reunion with Travis. Lisa had argued too long and fiercely nine years ago on his behalf. Better to let sleeping no-good insensitive dogs lie.

"Gram phoned a little earlier," Kara said instead. "Carol picked up from out by the register. By the time she turned the call over to me, she had Gram in a tizzy. I got a sound scolding on my failure to uphold the Taylor tradition of providing excellent customer service and employee working conditions."

"And in English that would mean...?"

"I had to let Jennifer go yesterday."

The part-time saleswoman had covered for Carol during her lunch hour, doctor's appointments and a slew of increasingly creative emergencies.

"Oh, hon, I'm sorry. I know how much help Jennifer was. How'd she take it?"

"Much better than Carol," Kara admitted wryly.

"O-o-ooh, I hate to see that lazy woman taking advantage of you." Lisa fingered the hammered

gold choker above her russet silk dress as if throt-
tling were on her mind. She cast a hostile glance at
the closed office door. "I wish you could've fired
her instead of Jennifer."

That made two of them.

But the middle-aged saleswoman had once been
best friends with her mother, and Gram treasured
and took comfort from the tenuous connection. Until that changed, Kara would put up with Carol's
sour disposition.

"Believe me," Kara assured her loyal friend,
"I'll hire more sales staff the minute I can divert
profits from *Mystery Woman* orders into the store.
Which, by the way, is the reason I agreed to set
Vinnie up on a blind date. He's going to print the
next catalogs at cost if I come through for him. I'll
save as much as four thousand dollars!"

"Why won't you let me give you—"

"*No.* It's bad enough I'm letting you do the photography free of charge. I won't accept your
money."

"Fine. Then accept a loan."

"Another debt hanging over my head? Thanks,
but no thanks." Kara pointedly checked her wrist-
watch. "You're going to be late to the country club
if you don't leave soon. Isn't your mother chairing
the fashion show luncheon this year?"

Irritation pinched Lisa's lovely features. She
snatched her purse from the floor and rose. "You

know she is. Just like you know she'll have a cow if I walk in late.''

She moved rigidly to the door, then paused dramatically, hand on the knob. "We're not finished, Kara. I'll stop by after the luncheon and you can tell me which proofs you want made into transparencies. And then maybe we'll discuss how the businesswoman Vinnie has talked to dozens of times and the *Mystery Woman* model he takes to dinner, are going to keep him from learning they're the same person!''

Tossing her dark chin-length bob, she flung open the door—and yelped.

Kara followed Lisa's gaze to the man standing with his knuckles raised as if to knock. Dark blond hair, impeccably tailored suit, wire-rim glasses that enhanced his Wall Street aura and polished good looks. He stared down with the dazed expression Kara had witnessed on masculine faces since the third grade.

No surprise, there.

The amazing thing was that Lisa stared up with an equally bemused look.

''Can I help you, sir?'' Kara asked, drawing his startled gaze.

He lowered his hand, his blue eyes sharpening. ''Ah, good. I wasn't completely sure you were the right Kara Taylor. May I speak with you, please?''

Probably a bill collector. ''I'm very busy.''

In a swift graceful movement, he placed both hands on Lisa's shoulders and reversed their positions. Oblivious to her outraged sputters, he smiled at Kara and stretched out a hand.

"Ross Hadley, producer, KLUV-TV. We *really* need to talk."

WATCHING PINE TREES flash by outside the Mercedes, Kara wondered if throwing up in Ross's direction would make him head back to Houston.

Not likely. Since meeting him four days ago, he'd displayed the annoying persistence of a Gulf Coast mosquito. If buzzing outlandish promises in her ears and sucking up her every objection hadn't fazed his conscience, a little vomit wouldn't make him squeamish. He was a man with a mission. And he'd finally convinced her that the ultimate benefits of pleading his cause were worth the risk of opening old wounds.

Of course, that had been yesterday. This morning she knew better.

Nothing was worth the nauseating tension growing stronger the closer they got to Lake Kimberly. Not the means to expand Mystery Woman, Inc.'s geographical reach and order-processing systems. Not the giddy thought of paying her most delinquent bills. Not the assurance that Gram could live out her life in the house she'd occupied for over fifty years...

Well, rats.

Kara was halfway into a deep calming breath when the scents of leather, Polo cologne and left-over Egg McMuffin hit her stomach. She concentrated grimly on the jazz music drifting from the radio until her queasiness eased.

Her problem, unfortunately, remained. No matter how much Gram cherished Taylor House, her stately home in The Heights, given a choice between declaring bankruptcy, or selling the valuable real estate to pay off business debts, she would choose the latter. Family honor was at stake.

Gram would live under the Pierce elevated bridge before tainting the Taylor name.

Like it or not, Kara's duty was clear. She would follow through on the original plan. Gaining an infusion of much-needed capital was worth losing her pride...and even her breakfast. A distinct possibility, given the challenge ahead.

Ross had invited Travis by phone to tape a pilot talk show with Kara. Her ex-husband had turned the first offer down flat. Also the second and third. Since he hung up now at the mere sound of Ross's voice, the TV producer thought a personal endorsement from Kara might make a difference.

He seemed to think that because Travis had never remarried, she'd retained a position of influence in his life. Ha! As if she'd ever been able to change Travis's mind.

A memory swooped out of hiding to mock her denial. *Travis, fending off her inexperienced kisses, resisting her timid touches, succumbing at last to her tearful pleas in a dark and musty boat shed. Building her passion quickly, loving her slowly, claiming her heart and soul forever—*

"You okay?" Ross asked, wrenching her into the present.

She blinked into focus. "Yes." A hideous suspicion made her add, "Why do you ask?"

"You moaned."

Through the blood rush of humiliation muffling her hearing, a saxophone wailed. "Sorry. Guess I'm not a big fan of Kenny G."

"Ahh. You should've said something earlier."

Sagging in relief, she watched him reach for the radio dial. The action strained his V-necked navy sweater across impressive shoulders, tightened his khaki slacks against muscular thighs. Tasseled loafers completed his interpretation of casual wear for their seventy-mile trip.

He settled on a classic rock station and leaned back, a *GQ* ad in the flesh. Good-looking, polished and successful. Eminently suitable.

For a moment, she tried to imagine herself with him in a musty boat shed.

"So, do I pass muster?" he asked, eyes on the road, his tone confident and slightly amused.

The truth disappointed her more than it would

him. "You don't really want or need my approval. You already know you're handsome. And you don't care what I think of your character, or else you would've backed off the first time I turned down your offer."

He cast her a wry look. "Ouch. You never pull any punches, do you?"

"Only around my grandmother," she admitted. "At least, I try to. I slip up every now and then. Last week at the *Vanessa Allen Show,* for example."

"I thought your grandmother was the show's biggest fan."

"She is."

"Wasn't she proud of how you acquitted yourself on national TV?"

Predictably, Gram had bragged about Kara in public and lectured her on decorum in private. "What entertains Gram on television, and how she expects her granddaughter to behave in life are worlds apart. And true ladies 'never display their tempers or speak rudely to others.'"

"Wow. What century is she living in?"

His tone was a little too condescending for Kara's liking. "Good manners never go out of style. At least, not in the *South.*"

He winced. "Ouch again. How long will I have to live here before you guys stop acting as if I'm a carpetbagger?"

She pretended to consider. "As soon as you start saying 'y'all' instead of 'you guys' without having to stop and think about it."

"I guess that means 'Yo!' won't cut it either, huh?"

Relenting, she smiled and shook her head.

"Did your grandmother really give you a hard time after the show?"

"It could've been much worse. Fortunately, her seeing Travis again took some of the heat off me."

"No love lost there, I'm sure."

"You're wrong. Gram *adored* Travis, and vice versa. From the time we separated until the divorce, she tried to talk me into returning to Lake Kimberly like a dutiful wife should. I swear she almost moved there herself so Travis would be well taken care of."

Ross chuckled, but Kara remembered those dark days too vividly to be amused. She'd…grieved was the only word to describe her anguish while waiting for him to make the first move that never came.

Eventually Gram and Lisa had ganged up, saying that if Kara wouldn't break down and talk to Travis, they would contact him and act as mediators. She'd lost it. Promised to leave Houston and never return if they so much as picked up the phone. It was the first—and last—time she'd ever screamed at either of them.

Shaken and pale, they'd agreed to respect her wishes.

"I've been divorced two years," Ross said quietly. "We weren't right for each other, but I still feel as if I flunked some major test to pass Life."

The moment of pained silence was oddly companionable.

When Kara dragged herself out of the doldrums, she felt a tenuous bond with the smooth producer. "You know, even if Travis agrees to do the pilot, I'll still have a battle on my hands with Gram. Unless..."

"I'm listening."

But would he understand? "She's been moping around the house too much lately. I'm so busy, it's hard for me to pinpoint the problem. Going to the *Vanessa Allen Show* was the first time I've seen her that excited in years. I think if she could feel involved somehow in the development stages of this pilot show, she wouldn't object so much to her granddaughter being a co-host."

"Hmm. I usually don't like too many fingers in the creative pie, but I'll give it some thought. I'd hate for you to have the additional stress of worrying about your grandmother. You'll have enough on your mind."

Oh, great. "Like how to keep from making a fool of myself?"

"Or me. I've got a lot riding on this show. Maybe my career."

"Thanks, Ross. You don't know how much better that makes me feel." She made a show of rubbing her temples. "Got any aspirin?"

"Not to worry. I'll coach you every step of the way. I won't let you get egg on your face, I promise."

Something in his twinkling gaze fixed carefully straight ahead made her flip down the visor mirror. A fleck of egg white and a few crumbs of Egg McMuffin clung to her chin.

"I'm doomed," she muttered, reaching for her purse and cosmetics. "Guess I should mention the shaving nick under your nose, huh?"

As she wiped her chin and applied fresh lipstick, her peripheral vision caught him tilting the rearview mirror to check his unblemished image. Raising her visor, she met his irritated glance and grinned.

He snorted and turned back to the road. Pushed up his glasses and draped a wrist over the steering wheel. Shook his head and slowly smiled. "Your poor grandmother has a shock in store when she discovers the real you."

Kara sobered. "Tell me about it. I pray she'll forgive me."

"For what? Being yourself? No offense, but it's time she got with the program. It's the new millennium. True ladies will get mowed down by real women who speak up for themselves. When you spar with Travis in the pilot, I want you to take off your gloves and use your fingernails if that's what it takes to make your point. The audience will love it. And the station will fund at least eight shows for sure.''

She had to laugh. ''You really are incorrigible.''

''So I've been told. Good thing I'm too cute to stay mad at.''

Amazingly, she believed him. Remembering Lisa's befuddled reaction to meeting Ross, Kara experienced a twinge of concern.

Watch out, girlfriend. This one is dangerous.

Not only cute, but also knowledgeable about still photography, if the high-dollar camera in the back seat was any indication. Together with video camcorder, tape recorder and remote microphone, the equipment prepared him for anything, he'd explained when Kara had commented earlier.

He leaned forward now and squinted through the windshield. ''We're looking for the Lake Kimberly exit, right?''

Her stomach took a nosedive. She followed his gaze to the upcoming I-45 sign. ''Our exit is about twenty miles ahead,'' she managed.

And to think she'd almost conquered her nausea.

Ross had gotten a friend to call the fishing camp that morning. Travis would supposedly be on the premises all day, and prospective guests could "stop by and give the place a look-see" any time. If she was lucky, the siren call of the lake had lured him out onto the water. He'd certainly heeded the call often enough during their marriage.

Glancing casually at Kara, Ross did a double take. "Hey, none of that, now. Don't wimp out on me."

She swallowed a hysterical laugh. "Now why would I wimp out? Just because my divorce was—" *devastating* "—not exactly amicable, and Travis already made it clear he thinks your plan is crazy doesn't mean he won't listen quietly to what I have to say and not kick me off the premises."

Ross reached over and patted her arm. "Don't worry. I'll be right there with you."

Travis will chew you up and spit you out for cat-fish bait. "I appreciate your chivalry, but I'd like to have a few minutes alone with him at first. I owe him that much, since he's not expecting us."

"Good thinking. You can smooth the way."

Kara simply nodded. Let the man have his illusions a bit longer.

Within a mile of leaving the interstate highway, she was hard pressed to give Ross accurate directions. The area had grown dramatically in the past nine years. Familiar landmarks had been camouflaged or replaced by encroaching development.

That Texaco station was new. As well as that

laundromat, convenience store and Fisherman's Cafe. Good heavens, Larry's Bait Shop was now a Dunkin' Donuts! How could that be? The ramshackle shop had been a local institution.

Her outrage retreated beneath an onslaught of guilt. Larry Royce would be around eighty years old now—if he was still alive. To her shame, she didn't know. When she'd left Lake Kimberly she'd severed all ties, including her link to Nancy, the gruff old fisherman's daughter. She'd been a good friend when Kara had needed one most.

Remorse joined the noose of emotion tightening slowly around her throat.

Closer to the lake, the towering pines she remembered so well littered the winding blacktop road with rusty needles and crushed cones. The handful of vacation homes she'd passed daily on her way to and from Houston still remained. What had once seemed like palaces were actually modest structures, she realized now.

Yet their aged condition and small size weren't what shocked Kara. No, it was the neighboring houses that blew her away.

She gaped at the new fences, many constructed of elaborate wrought iron or imposing brick, that guarded private lakefront showplaces shimmering through the trees. Travis had always said Houston's well-to-do would discover Lake Kimberly one day.

How he must loathe the modern castles that,

rather than blending naturally into their setting, shouted visually for attention.

"Slow down," she croaked to Ross. "We should be getting close to the turnoff soon."

"You sure? This doesn't look like 'a godforsaken frontier settlement' to me."

Heat stung her cheeks. Her favorite description of the area sounded shrewish within sight of veritable mansions.

"Things have changed along the access road," she admitted. "Wait'll we get to the fishing camp itself."

Intense curiosity wove through her dread. What changes would she find? There were bound to be a lot after so many years, even if Travis had kept his vow to impact the lake's ecosystem as little as possible.

"There!" She nodded toward a small sign mounted above a battered blue mailbox.

Ross drove close and shifted into park, leaving the engine idling.

The words Bass Busters Fishing Camp topped a directional arrow pointing to a sagging aluminum gate. On the other side, two gravel ruts disappeared into woods wilder and thicker than any they'd passed. It was hard to imagine a person on foot getting through unscathed, much less a luxury automobile.

Turning off the radio, Ross looked from the gate to Kara. "You're kidding."

"I tried to tell you. Lord knows how clients find Travis." If, in fact, he had any clients left for his fishing guide service, the stubborn fool. "He never did listen to me about the importance of advertising and first impressions."

Frowning, she studied the faded sign, the drooping barbed wire fence, the closed gate and wilderness beyond.

"Well, he listened to somebody," Ross said thoughtfully. "His answering machine gives a web site address for Bass Busters Fishing Camp. I checked it out."

Kara whipped her head around.

"He's booked through next July as a guide. The man's almost a legend, Kara. You could've at least told me."

She closed her mouth. "Legend?"

He removed his glasses and cleaned the lenses with a bit of shirt, his sea-blue eyes both vaguer and sharper than before. "Boy, when you divorce someone, you really move on, don't you? Your ex-husband has won every major bass-fishing tournament in Texas. He caught the record largemouth bass in the state two years ago. His list of published magazine articles is damned impressive."

"Magazine articles?"

Ross slipped on his glasses and cocked his head.

"We'll have to work on that echo before the pilot, Kara. But yes, when it comes to bass fishing in Texas, Travis Malloy is a top player."

The emotion choking her now was dangerously close to pride. She flung open her door and slid out.

"I'll open the gate," she said, slamming the door on his astonished expression.

Kara trudged to the disreputable hunk of metal, shoved the bolt aside, then pushed the sagging gate forward. By the time she'd plowed a long enough furrow to allow room for the Mercedes to pass through, she'd regained a safe measure of irritation.

So Travis had done well for himself. Why shouldn't he have earned a reputation as a great fishing guide? The man had been obsessed with the slimy creatures, after all.

If he'd put half as much effort into understanding her as he had into deciphering bass feeding patterns, she wouldn't have fled the fishing camp crying so hard she could barely see to drive away.

The return drive now would be different, Kara promised herself, wrestling the gate shut and ramming the bolt home. She wasn't a defenseless broken-hearted girl anymore, but a mature capable woman. She could handle whatever lay ahead, and then some.

Holding tightly to that thought, she walked to the car and slipped inside. She continued holding tightly throughout the winding drive through dense forest. As the Mercedes broke into the five-acre clearing Travis had christened Bass Busters Fishing Camp, she clutched her righteous courage even tighter—a puny shield against the merciless pounding of her heart.

It hadn't changed at all!

There were the five one-room log cabins scattered to the left of the clapboard and fieldstone house. There was the long pier capped by a rusting tin boat shed, and the cement launch ramp lapped by gentle shoreline waves.

And there—oh rats—there, glittering a shade deeper than the cloudless sky, extending as far as the eye could see across the horizon, was a magnificent faceted sapphire reflecting the October sunshine.

Lake Kimberly, her beautiful enemy.

Kara schooled her features into a mask of indifference, hoping her turtleneck would hide her frantic pulse. If it killed her, she wouldn't reveal the power of either this place—or its owner—to hurt her again.

CHAPTER FOUR

TRAVIS UNLOCKED the boat-shed door, slipped inside and waited for his eyes to adjust from the bright sunshine. Built straddling the end of a fifty-foot pier, the structure sheltered eight boat slips—four on each side of the "dock"—and a large workbench and tool cabinet against the far wall.

The single large window might've provided adequate light minus the layer of grunge coating the lakeside glass. One more chore he never got around to starting. Putting out fires claimed most of his time.

Turning his Evinrude cap backward, he headed for the latest sorry piece of junk to go up in flames: a nine-horsepower outboard motor on one of his four aluminum skiffs. At the last slip on his left, he stepped down from the dock into the boat.

The day before, a lawyer and his ten-year-old son had stalled out in this skiff at about noon. When Travis had returned at three from fishing the lake's northern points, he'd had an uneasy feeling that the two were in trouble. At four, he'd set out in search of the pair and found them at six—hungry and pan-icked—far down the isolated southern shore.

That was one customer who wouldn't help the camp's reputation any. The fact he was a lawyer *really* helped. Sheesh. All Travis needed was a screwy lawsuit to make his life complete.

Shaking his head in disgust, he set the throttle on neutral, pumped the primer and yanked the starter cord. Water bubbled and boiled. The engine smoked, sputtered and spit.

And Travis spewed out a stream of curses.

Only last spring, he'd overhauled each skiff's an-cient outboard, plus his tournament Skeeter's 150-horsepower Yamaha. Yet all five motors had malfunctioned periodically throughout the busy summer. This current mechanical failure sounded like a compression problem.

Perfect. More lost rental income. More time spent wielding tools instead of a fishing rod.

He cut the engine, resentment spreading through him like the oily foam above the stilled propeller.

Bass Busters Fishing Camp was supposed to have freed him to do what he loved most, not trap him into a life of indentured servitude. He hadn't spent years studying bass behavior and how it re-lated to a lake's structure and cover only to piddle away the prime of his life on tedious grease-monkey jobs.

Damn, but he was tired of jerking around with

repairs! Tired of exhaust fumes, creosote and latent mildew filling his lungs. Tired of this ramshackle tin-roofed boat shed blocking wide Texas skies and cool lake breezes.

Lately if he wasn't in here sweating, he was outside on the campgrounds sweating even more. Hell, he'd had to withdraw from the Sam Rayburn tournament last month when Cabin Three's septic tank backed up. Talk about stinky luck!

Snorting a laugh, Travis wiped his brow with the hem of his cropped-sleeved sweatshirt. All his grand plans for this place had wound up in the toilet. Oh, he'd developed a customer base for the camp, all right. But not the substructure to service it. Traveling to tournaments and guiding clients left little time to do more than crisis management.

Kara had predicted as much nine years ago....

Travis lowered his sweatshirt.

Her again. The real reason for his foul mood and discontent. He'd slept lousy since seeing Kara last week, and not at all since helping take inventory at Malloy Sporting Goods store the night before.

Enlisting Nancy for the chore as well, he'd let the fishing camp take care of itself. Cameron had left his ad agency clients in Austin to join them. Seth had trusted his veterinary practice in Wagner to an assistant and driven in. And Jake, who worked full-time with their dad in the store, had tormented them all with bad jokes and ceaseless clowning. The usual routine.

Taking inventory had become a sacred annual tradition. The one guaranteed night of the year all the Malloy men were under one roof.

Bending to rummage in the toolbox at his feet, Travis admitted he'd been a tad touchy to begin with. Then the inevitable happened. Despite threats of bodily harm, Jake had described Kara and Travis's TV debut to Cameron, who'd squealed to Seth, who'd snitched to Dad, who'd blabbed to Nancy.

His brothers, to a man, had been smitten with Kara and opposed to the divorce. They would've interfered at the separation stage if Travis hadn't said a line had been drawn, and it was up to her to step over to his side. He'd vowed, dead serious, never to forgive the Malloy who approached Kara. Even Jake had believed him.

But last night, the brothers had decided fate had given Travis a second chance to correct his bone-head mistake.

Only his father, who'd never remarried in the twenty years since Kathryn Malloy's death, had advised Travis to keep his distance from Kara and leave the past buried. Divorce was almost like having a spouse die, after all.

Frowning, he shook off the thought, lifted a

wrench from his toolbox and turned to the problem at hand.

Minutes later he cocked his head as car doors slammed. The dentists booked for Cabin Two? Whoever was here, Nancy would have to show them around. In one smooth movement, Travis hoisted the detached motor from the boat onto the dock.

Uh-oh.

Ver-ry gingerly, he clambered up himself, then knuckled the shooting pain in his lower back. Defending his I-Am-Sibling-King title in the store's home gym section had taken its toll. A small price to pay for keeping his brothers humble.

The sound of footsteps killed his smirk. Someone was heading up the wood-plank pier. Fast. He turned, his senses on high alert. The door twenty feet away burst open.

Nancy Royce jogged inside, dressed in jeans and a Tweety Bird T-shirt, her dark ponytail swaying. Despite looking more like a college coed than a woman twelve years his senior, she commanded his full respect and attention. Hiring her after Larry died had been the smartest business move he'd ever made.

"You have visitors," she announced as she neared, her gaze sweeping his thong sandals, cutoff jeans and cropped sweatshirt critically.

She stopped close enough for him to read anxious excitement in her gray eyes. "I can try and stall them while you go shower and change—and scrape that stubble off your face. Put on the cologne I gave you for Christmas."

His skin prickled in warning. A second pair of feet now walked the pier.

"Oh, Lord, she didn't wait," Nancy blurted, confirming his premonition. "Brace yourself, Travis. Kara wants to talk to you."

His pulse leaped first, his gaze second, landing on the silhouette framed in the doorway.

Staring at the maturation of youthful promise walking toward him, Travis found himself searching for something—anything—that didn't please him.

No luck in her form-fitting black pants and turtleneck. His gaze lifted desperately. She'd twisted up and clipped her hair with a tortoiseshell gizmo, the style flattering her high cheekbones, wide-set eyes and long aristocratic nose.

He liked her hair better down.

She'd applied dramatic cherry-red lipstick to her kiss-me mouth, the color emphasizing her pale smooth complexion and small stubborn chin.

He liked her lips better naked.

She'd lost the air of demure innocence he'd first admired and then protected at a rowdy fraternity party. This older Kara appeared worldly and confident. In charge of herself and her surroundings.

Able to handle a tipsy football player or any other man who dared try to intimidate her or stand in her way.

He liked her better helpless and grateful.

A sudden image of Kara surrounded by macho jerks slapped his conscience.

Okay, not helpless. But the new assertiveness he'd noticed last week wasn't...ladylike. Yeah, that's what had been bugging him. The old Kara never would've "dissed her man" in private, much less on national television.

Earth to Malloy, an inner voice jeered. *You're not her man anymore.*

Nancy smiled a welcome as Kara stopped.

Her spicy floral perfume wafted onward—a fragrance that had lingered longest in the deep folds of her abandoned robe. He'd sniffed the silk like it was glue until he'd finally had to burn the thing to break his sick addiction.

Kara reached out and squeezed Nancy's forearm briefly. "I'm glad to see your head's still intact. Thanks for braving the lion in his den."

Nancy chuckled. "No problem."

Travis felt oafish, dirty and snarling mean. "I wouldn't be too sure of that."

Kara met his gaze, her expression cooling rapidly.

Once upon a time those uptilted eyes, the impenetrable green of a quiet pond, had been the proverbial window to her soul. Now Travis was forced to guess her thoughts. Another change he didn't like.

"Hello, Travis. Could I speak to you a minute?"

He'd waited twelve friggin' months after she'd left him to hear that question. And then it had been to announce she wanted a divorce. "I'm kinda busy right now. Why don't you check back with me in, say, another eight years or so?"

"Tra-vis," Nancy admonished.

"Hey, *I'm* not the one out of line here, Nancy. She should've called first and made an appointment. Even this 'godforsaken frontier settlement' has a phone." From the heightened color in Kara's cheeks, his dart had hit bull's-eye.

Funny, how little satisfaction he felt.

Unable to meet either woman's gaze, he leaned down, grasped the outboard motor and swung it up to his chest. Sharp pain stabbed his lower back. Hissing in a breath, he turned and headed grimly for the workbench.

"Want me to bring you more Ben-Gay?" Nancy asked, her tone deceptively sweet.

He stiffened and paused, then continued forward without answering.

Kara picked up the dropped ball. "Why does he need Ben-Gay?"

"He and his brothers helped John with inventory last night."

"Ahhh." Obviously she remembered the annual competition. "Who won?"

Travis jerked the motor upright between clamps and began tightening the vise.

"That depends entirely on who you ask. Each brother says he did. But my money's on Jake."

The motor's casing cracked ominously. Travis loosened the clamps a fraction.

"You're probably right," Kara murmured. "I couldn't help noticing how much he's filled out since I last saw him. He's as big as Travis now. And of course, he *is* six years younger."

"True."

Travis whirled around and stalked forward, ready to defend his title.

Feminine laughter, the indulgent kind that made a man feel eight years old, penetrated his outrage. Heat burned slowly up his neck.

Nancy pat-patted his arm. "I was only teasing, sweetie. But now that the ice is broken, I'll just leave you two alone." She headed for the door, calling over her shoulder, "Mr. Hadley and I will be in the office if you need us."

Hadley? The name clicked as she ducked outside. Travis turned to Kara and folded his arms.

Her gaze skittered across his chest. "The place hasn't changed a bit since I left," she murmured.

His ego flinched. He watched her turn in a slow

lazy circle, scanning the shed's interior as if absorbing every detail.

She was remembering his promise to build a larger boat shed in "about three years, four years tops." She was remembering his similar promise to build new guest cabins to replace the ones outside. She was remembering his big talk of building a 150-foot fishing pier next to the boat ramp.

Her lashes suddenly fluttered, her cheeks flushed, her lips parted, her hand lifted to her throat. Following her transfixed stare to his fifteen-year-old Skeeter bass rig, he stopped breathing.

She was remembering the first time they'd made love.

His body stirred. He catapulted back to the night she'd appeared in his boat shed, chaste but eager, sweetly passionate, obliterating his noble plan to court her slowly, as a true lady deserved. God help him, he'd taken her virginity atop a cushioned bait well, then continued her education during the following weeks. They'd been crazy in love—or so he'd thought. One month after meeting her, he'd made her his wife.

One year after that, he'd followed his nose to a charred rack of lamb, shriveled green beans, crusty baked potatoes and lopsided chocolate cake. He'd eyed the tablecloth, wilted flowers, and short stubs of tall tapered candles. He'd known she was gone, and he'd almost thrown up.

Travis yanked his thoughts into the present. "I've got work to do, Kara. What's on your mind?"

Her startled glance and deepening blush confirmed she hadn't been admiring the boat's sleek lines. *Damn,* why couldn't she have stayed in his past?

He lowered his brows. "If you drove out here with Hadley to talk about some cockamamie TV talk show, you wasted your time. I already told him I wouldn't do it."

"I'm—" She stopped and cleared her throat. "I'm aware of that. But you've got to admit that the money he's offering is quite generous."

"I don't need his money," Travis lied.

"Frankly, Travis, I do. Or rather, Taylor Fine Foundations does. The store is in trouble."

Store? As in singular? He hid his shock behind a veneer of sarcasm. "Frankly, my dear, I don't give a damn."

Her eyes frosted. "You never did."

"That's bull and you know it! But if you're saying I cared *more* about Bass Busters Fishing Camp…damn right I did. This place was my livelihood, our future children's security."

The children they'd both wanted and specified. A brown-eyed boy with dark hair for her. A green-eyed girl with fair hair for him. So clichéd it was laughable. Only he didn't feel like laughing.

For a hideous horrifying instant, his nose stung.

Her expression thawed. "And Taylor Fine Foundations was my legacy," she said quietly. "Something of value *I* could pass on to our children."

Welcoming the insult to his pride, he braced his hands on his hips. "I could sell this property tomorrow for a half-million dollars, easy. That's right," he addressed the surprise in her eyes with vindicated satisfaction. "You should've trusted me that lakefront real estate value would go through the roof one day."

"I never doubted you, Travis."

Ignoring that whopper, he slid his hands into his pockets and rocked back on his heels. "Yep, the fish you threw back could've made you rich. If only you'd known."

Not that he would ever sell a square inch of his land while he drew breath.

But she didn't know that.

A delicate brow arched. "You'd never sell this land. I'd have to wait until your flaming funeral pyre floated off into the sunset before I saw a penny."

As kids, he and his brothers had made a secret blood vow to give each other proper Viking funerals when they croaked. "How'd you…?"

She leveled a "get real" look.

"Jake," he muttered darkly.

"Besides—" she folded her arms beneath her

breasts ''—I didn't marry *or* divorce you for money. Half this property was legally mine. Don't think my lawyer didn't advise me to take it, either. Or that I wouldn't have won if you'd fought me on it.''

''I wouldn't have fought.'' Travis couldn't have been more surprised had a Jack-in-the-box popped out of his mouth.

''You wouldn't?'' Her arms relaxed slightly. Confusion furrowed her smooth brow.

''No. I always wondered why you didn't ask for your fair share.''

''Because *any* share wouldn't have been fair.'' She offered a small rueful smile. ''I was pretty useless as far as helping you was concerned.''

Perversely angry, Travis frowned down at his thongs and bare feet, long narrow things she'd once called submarines. ''Why are you telling me this now?''

''I told you then. Over and over. But you never *heard* me. I needed to feel productive. Gram was over her head managing the company, and I could be a true help. I could maybe save a business that had been in my family for over seventy years. You didn't understand how important that was to me.''

An upsurge of resentment lifted his head. ''Sure I did. It was more important than putting up with bad plumbing and loud-mouthed fishermen at 6:00 a.m. It was more important than scheduling guide trips or cleaning cabins or mucking out rental skiffs. It was more important than being home when I walked in tired from a long day…and hungry.'' *For you,* the sexual growl in his voice said.

Somehow he'd moved close enough to see heat ripple across her pond-green eyes. Her dizzying floral scent tugged his nose lower.

"Gram needed me more than you needed sex," she said distinctly.

Travis jerked back as if slapped.

Her Ice Queen persona was fully in place. "I needed to feel like a wife, not a concubine."

Swearing ripely he turned, walked to an empty gas tank perched on the edge of the pier and hooked two fingers in the handle. Gram needed. Kara needed. His emotions churned as he carried the rusting metal toward his workbench.

Well, *he'd* needed to feel close to his wife. And toward the end of their first year of marriage, sex was the one form of communication left to him that produced a brief sense of intimacy. Though her reserved modesty was always an initial barrier, his patience was well rewarded after she caught fire.

If he hadn't initiated lovemaking, he and Kara might as well have lived on Mars and Venus, respectively. They sure as hell hadn't been able to talk without getting tangled up in hurt feelings.

Maybe there was something to Hadley's concept for a new TV show, after all.

Travis set the gas tank next to his toolbox and turned around, his backside propped against the workbench. "Look, even if I wanted to make a fool of myself on TV, I couldn't take the time. I've got the camp to run."

Her eyes widened. She lowered her arms and walked forward excitedly. "Tuesday and Wednesday are your slowest days. Ross has already agreed to rehearse and tape then."

"I don't know..."

"If the pilot takes off, we'd only have to commit to seven or eight shows. Surely we can get along for that amount of time?"

After the emotions she'd dredged up, Travis was pretty damn sure they'd have a problem. "I've got guide trips scheduled for months. A lot of them are with new clients."

"You'd make triple what you'd earn taking clients out on the lake, so if you did have to cancel, it wouldn't matter."

That was one of the biggest sources of their marital disharmony. She'd *never* thought canceling out on clients mattered.

"If I cancel on first-time clients, another guide will get their business—and nine times out of ten, their repeat business, too."

"Maybe. But in the long run, you'll recoup any losses through the capital improvements you'll be able to make." She swept an eloquent nose-wrinkled look over his sorry fleet of boats.

So she *had* remembered his grand promises. And obviously judged him lacking for not keeping them.

"Forget it, Kara. I'm not interested."

"But...I don't understand."

"Go back to Houston and find another chump to interpret the male point of view. And in case you don't understand *that,* let me translate for you."

He straightened from the workbench and set both hands at his waist. "I wouldn't co-host a show with you if my life depended on it. Is that clear enough?"

"Perfectly." Every trace of color had blanched from her cheeks.

He ignored his sharp twinge of conscience. "Good."

She lifted her chin. "But what if *Gram's* life depended on it?"

CHAPTER FIVE

WHEN TRAVIS PALED beneath his tan, Kara hastened to add, "Not literally, of course. But you remember Gram and her sense of Taylor pride. It will kill her spirit to see the last store close. She'll think she failed to preserve our family heritage."

A dull flush of anger replaced Travis's pallor.

"Still using emotional blackmail to get your way, eh, Kara? Why don't you just tell the truth? *You're* the one who'd be crushed if the last store closes. 'Cause that would mean you couldn't cut it as a wife *or* a businesswoman."

Kara flinched, then turned and headed for fresh air that didn't reek of bitterness.

"Kara, wait!"

She kept walking, her one focused thought to get to the car and away from this man whose power to wound her was as strong as ever. A foot away from the door, he grabbed her shoulder from behind and spun her around.

"Damn it, Kara, I'm sorry! I didn't mean that. But what am I supposed to think when you manipulate me with some sob story about your grand-mother?''

"I don't know, Travis. Maybe that I'm telling the truth?''

Facing the light, his thickly lashed eyes were a tortoiseshell mixture of dark- and amber-brown. Beautiful, except for their gleam of suspicion.

Kara's heart twisted. "It's not the store closing that I'm most worried about. Unless cash flow improves, I'll have to sell Taylor House and everything inside it. And that *will* devastate Gram.''

Travis had been given the grand tour. He'd seen Gram proudly show off each room and recite the family history behind each piece of furniture and knickknack, from valuable antiques to the lumpy clay pot Kara had made in fourth-grade art class. He knew Pamela Taylor's bedroom was exactly as she'd left it twenty-six years ago, and that Gram found comfort touching her daughter's possessions.

His shocked expression reflected that knowledge. "Are things really that bad?''

Humble pie had never tasted so foul. "Yes, Travis. They're that bad.''

If she hadn't been watching him so closely, she might've missed the tiny flicker of triumph in his eyes.

"I never should have come here,'' she admitted, turning to plunge through the door into the sunlight and continue down the pier.

His sandals slapped close at her heels. "So why did you?"

"Because I'm stupid. Because I never learn. Because I thought you wouldn't penalize Gram for being related to me—o-oh, *never mind*." Eyes straight ahead, she sped up. "It's pointless to talk to you. You still don't *listen*."

"And you still run away when things get sticky."

Kara stopped cold.

Two hundred and ten pounds of muscle and bone kept going, slamming into her back. She stumbled forward and hit the pier as if launching onto a Slip 'n' Slide.

Stunned, she inhaled the biting scent of sun-warmed creosote, registered the heat and uneven surface of plank boards, tasted the coppery tang of blood an instant before pain made her hiss in a breath.

"Kara! Oh, damn, are you all right?" Travis sounded satisfyingly worried.

His powerful hands lifted and turned her until she was half-sitting, her head lolling back against the rock pillow of his rounded biceps.

She squinted up at his fearsome scowl, noting irrelevantly that his beard was heavier than that of the twenty-four-year-old she'd married. His features were harder and bolder, too, the result, intensely masculine. Much sexier than handsome.

"Aw, jeez, Kara, your mouth is bleeding. You must've bitten it when your chin hit." He pressed a thumb pad gently on her lower lip, feathered an index finger over her stinging chin, brushed the back of his knuckles down her cheek.

Those magic hands. Strong enough to open the tightest vacuum-sealed jar, yet capable of touching her as gently as moth wings. For a moment only, she promised herself, she would enjoy the luxury of feeling safe and fussed over.

"Let me see your palms," he ordered.

Like an obedient child, she raised them for his inspection.

His muttered oath was at odds with the tender concern in his eyes. "Can you walk, honey?"

Honey.

Kara melted, then stiffened. She wasn't his honey. Nor was she helpless, though he'd always liked to think her so.

She sat up so fast her head clipped his chin. He yelped and jerked back, his whiskers pulling fine strands of blond hair with him.

"Sorry," she mumbled. Scrambling to her feet, she assessed the damage.

Her right palm had snagged several jagged splinters while leaving flesh behind. Her left was better, but the pinky knuckle was scraped and would probably scab over, darn it. Lisa would have to do some creative framing in the final catalog shots.

Probing her tender chin and lip, Kara was thankful the Mystery Woman's face was never photographed directly.

"C'mon, Kara, let's go up to the house and get those hands disinfected," Travis said in a tone brooking no argument.

He grabbed her elbow, but she dug in her heels. "Wait. Before I see Ross, I need to know if you'll agree to do a pilot or not. There's no sense stringing him along if you have no intention of saying yes."

Every trace of tenderness vanished from Travis's face. "Funny. You didn't have a moral problem stringing *me* along for a year before saying no to a reconciliation."

Kara gaped, then yanked her arm away. "You never *asked* me for a reconciliation."

"I sure as hell never asked for a divorce."

Quivering with outrage, she glared at his sullen expression. "You never talked about our marriage problems, period. You were too hardheaded to go to counseling. That was for couples who shouldn't be together in the first place, remember? So don't pull that whiny wounded martyr act on me, Travis Malloy."

He puffed up. "I am *not* whiny."

His petulant tone rang out over the water with startling clarity. Chagrin crept into his eyes.

The absurdity of the situation struck Kara.

There they stood, arguing like children on a playground about an endeavor whose success depended on their facilitating communication between the sexes. It was too ironic, too ridiculous for words. She sputtered.

"You think this is funny?"

Laughing outright, Kara nodded. How had she ever thought she could work with Travis on such a show? Talk about the blind leading the blind!

"Wanna share the joke?"

"Look at us," she chortled. "You're right to say no to co-hosting a show with me. I'd bash your brains in with my microphone and wind up on death row."

An expression she'd never seen before replaced his irritation.

"I doubt it," he said.

"Well, don't. We women of the new millennium are more aggressive than ever."

"Yeah, but we martyrs are too hardheaded to get our brains bashed in."

Kara hooted. "Good point. Bet I could make you whine, though."

That strange gleam in his eyes intensified. His mouth curved up in a grudging smile. "I don't like the odds on that bet. Now, what do you say we get those cuts of yours taken care of?"

He took her elbow and steered her firmly into a walk. "Esther wouldn't approve of you calling me names, Kara Ann."

"You started it," she grumbled.

"Did not."

"Did so."

"Did not."

"Did *so*."

"Did so,"

"Did n—" She narrowed her eyes at his devilish grin. "You know, Travis Dean, for nine years I've actually maintained a reasonable degree of maturity and dignity. Some people even think of me as an adult."

"I'm sure they do, honey. But have you had any fun?"

She opened and closed her mouth, surprised to realize they'd stopped at the end of the pier.

Had she had any fun?

Kara thought back to the agonizing year of their separation, the equally painful months after their divorce. She thought of missing his brothers' teasing and bickering, his father's quiet authority, the dynamics of a large boisterous family so different from her own. She thought of the years flowing one into another as work became her reason for getting up in the morning, her excuse for having no social life.

The men she'd dated were never as arrogant, never as annoying...never as much fun as Travis.

"No," she admitted in a small voice. "I don't suppose I have."

The concern was back in his eyes.

Her urge to move closer and lean on his strength was so utterly compelling she turned and stepped off the pier instead. Her shaky legs buckled, but he was there instantly to offer support. They started up the slope to the main house.

Three times during the climb she slipped on the slick grass. With every stumble, she grew more aware of subtle changes in the man beside her.

He was taller than she remembered. Craning her neck was disconcerting after years of facing most men eye-to-eye. He seemed bigger to her in general, though not an ounce of fat contributed to the impression. The bare arm she'd grabbed was like warm granite, the stomach beneath his cropped sweatshirt flat and rippled, his chest wide and deep. He'd gained muscle mass in the nine years since she'd touched him last.

Kara suddenly wondered who touched him now. "I visited a bit with Nancy earlier. I was sorry to hear that Larry died, but she must be a huge help to you."

"Nancy?" Travis seemed to have difficulty pulling his thoughts together. "Yeah, Nancy's great. I don't know what I'd do without her managing the office. Last year when I had the flu, she even took some of my clients out on the lake. Hell, Stan Palmer caught a seven-pounder and thinks she's the greatest thing since sliced bread."

Apparently Stan wasn't the only one. "She seems happy working for you. Does she commute from Conroe?"

"No. You remember George Weller, don't you?"

Kara struggled to place the name.

"You know, he used to come inspect the day's catch, try to pump my clients for point locations?"

Knowledge of prime bass hangouts, "points" formed by rocks and mud coupled with grass or trees, were a fishing guide's most valuable asset.

"O-oh, *that* George. How could I forget?" Travis had griped daily about his elderly neighbor. "What about him?"

"His rheumatism got so bad he had to stop fishing. But he can't bear to sell the cottage, so Nancy rents it now. Works out great since she can just walk over to my place."

Kara mustered a weak smile. "How convenient." They were nearing the house. Not much time left. "I didn't see a wedding ring on her finger. I'm surprised she never got married." At his sharp glance, she added, "Or did she?"

His expression grew shuttered. "No."

Hmm. "What happened with Joey Harrison?" When she'd left, he and Nancy were a hot item.

"That's not my business to tell."

Kara's cheeks stung. She'd deserved that. Her

flush deepened when the front door opened and Nancy's head popped out.

"Oh, Travis, good. I was just on my way to talk to you."

He released Kara's elbow and tensed. "Anything wrong?"

"Dr. Moore phoned a minute ago. He wants to reschedule tomorrow's trip for another day, unless you're going to charge him a cancellation fee—in which case he'll drive on out late tonight."

"You gotta be kiddin'!" Travis blew out a peeved breath. "Like he cut me a break on my porcelain crown last month."

Nancy shrugged sympathetically. "I told him you'd call back within the hour." Her dove-gray gaze moved to Kara and widened. "Oh, my gosh! Come in, come in."

The older woman opened the door wider, stood aside to let them pass and caught her breath. "Kara, your beautiful hands. What happened?"

But Kara was swamped in nostalgia and couldn't respond.

They'd entered a spacious living area bounded on the right by a large fieldstone fireplace, and on the left by two bedroom doors, one of them open. She glimpsed the corner of a battered office desk before turning to scan her favorite room in the house.

The same faded blue sofa faced the hearth, its

cushions sagging even more than when she'd seen them last. The same folded white afghan draped one arm.

She walked thoughtfully to the sofa and fingered the bedraggled blanket. Soft wonder thickened her throat.

Gram's hand-knitted birthday gift to Travis had obviously meant more to him than she'd realized. Lifting a corner of the afghan, Kara saw that the dime-sized threadbare spot it used to cover was now the size of a quarter.

"My God, Kara, did he actually hit you?"

She dropped the blanket. Her gaze snapped to the office doorway, where Ross stood staring at her mouth. She looked at Travis, who seemed to have grown a couple of inches.

Rats.

"Did I *what?*" Travis asked.

Nancy moved close, laid a restraining hand on his forearm and shot Ross a distressed look.

Mr. Producer slipped smoothly back into place. "Forgive me. That was inexcusably rude. The thing is, I've been sitting here getting more and more worried about Kara, and when I saw her lip…"

He walked toward Travis with a conciliatory expression. "I knew you were pretty burned about the idea of co-hosting a talk show, and she'd told me you wouldn't want to talk to her. I jumped to an unforgivable conclusion, but I hope you'll accept my apology." He stopped an arm's length away and extended his hand. "Ross Hadley, KLUV-TV."

Travis slowly folded his arms across his chest.

Ross's affable smile fell along with his hand. "Nice to meet you."

Travis grunted. "If you thought there was even a remote chance I could hit Kara, why the hell did you let her talk to me alone?"

To Ross's credit, his blue gaze never wavered. "You're right. I *should* have gone with her. Again, I apologize."

"Excuse me," Kara said, waggling her fingers. "I believe I insisted on talking to Travis alone. No apology is necessary."

Neither man so much as flicked a glance her way.

Travis lowered his brows at the producer. "Your first mistake was dragging Kara here to do your dirty work."

Ross drew himself up. "I didn't drag her. She came willingly. Kara's got a vested interest in this meeting."

"Yoo-hoo?" Kara waved her hand broadly, to no avail.

"Your *second* mistake was not taking what I said over the phone seriously. Just what part of 'no way in hell' don't you understand?"

"You hung up before I could lay out the whole proposal. We owed it to you to drive out here—"

"Guys!" Kara bellowed, capturing three startled gazes. She waited until the men were one hundred percent with her. "If you two don't stop talking as if I'm invisible, I can't be responsible for the consequences."

Nancy laughed and nodded approvingly.

Encouraged, Kara focused on the main culprit. "Nobody dragged me here, Travis. Ross and I felt an obligation to give you all the details before you made a final decision. But you know what I've decided? *You* have an obligation to listen to *us*. The stakes are too high—for too many other people—for you not to extend us that courtesy."

She trailed a finger lightly and deliberately over the afghan.

Travis's mouth tightened as her reminder of Gram hit home.

"So here's the deal," Kara continued. "We're all going to sit down and have a civilized discussion. Ross, you'll stick to the facts and leave out the sales pitch. Travis, you'll keep an open mind. Nancy…I'd appreciate it if you'd be the mediator."

"Really?" Nancy broke into a delighted smile. "I'd enjoy that. But first, your hands and mouth have got to be stinging. Why don't we go into the kitchen and fix you up before we start?"

Kara remembered why she'd liked the older woman so much all those years ago. "That would be *wonderful.*"

"Not so fast," Travis warned in an ominous tone, stopping Kara in her tracks. "We all have our orders. But you haven't said what *you're* going to do during this 'civilized' discussion."

She flashed an evil grin. "I'm going to hold the microphone. There's one in the back seat of the Mercedes. Ask Ross if you don't believe me."

That strange gleam, a kind of bemused fascination, reappeared in Travis's eyes. He cocked a brow at Ross. "She telling the truth?"

Clearly baffled, Ross nodded. "But don't worry, we're not going to tape the meeting. Kara's being a little overzealous. I'll talk to her before we start."

Travis snorted. "Better stop acting like she's invisible, pal. I can't stand to see a grown man whine."

CHAPTER SIX

NINETY MINUTES LATER, Nancy sat at the kitchen table in silent admiration as Kara added the capper to her closing argument.

"Okay, forget the money you'd earn to make improvements to the camp. Forget your heightened name recognition that could only help attract sponsors for national fishing tournaments. Forget the fact that you'd keep a sweet old lady from getting kicked out of the home she loves. Travis, do you have any idea how valuable your local celebrity status could be to Malloy Sporting Goods?"

"I'm not following you."

"When you helped with inventory last night, did you or Cameron or Seth notice a decrease in the amount of stock the store is carrying?"

Watching the stubborn Malloy pride keep Travis mute, Nancy spoke up. "I did. John doesn't talk about it much, but the new Oshman's Super Store that opened last year has really cut into his business." Ignoring her employer's betrayed expression, she shared a worried look with Kara. "Frankly, I was shocked at the skimpy selection.

I'm no marketing expert, and I know he's trying to cut costs, but it seems to me that's the worst response right now. People who *do* walk in won't find what they need and will head straight for Oshman's—'' Nancy flashed a rebellious glance at Travis ''—no matter *how* good the service is.''

Kara looked sympathetic. ''Unfortunately, you're probably right. When a retailer is losing business— and money—sometimes spending more on advertising and inventory is the best way to retain market share. It's a scary strategy to implement, though.''

Ross picked up the ball. ''And you'd want to get the most bang from your advertising dollar. See, Travis, if the show takes off, you could endorse your father's store in an advertising campaign and make a difference. You'd be a natural. I mean, you practically grew up in the store, right? Working there after school and on weekends, shooting the breeze with customers, developing your own version of an in-store Iron Man contest for all the Malloys.''

Travis slanted a dark look at Kara.

Ross shook his head. ''Don't blame her. She wouldn't tell me anything. Your brother's the one who filled me in. Didn't he mention I spoke with him a couple of days ago?''

Travis flipped off his Evinrude cap and finger-combed his hair. ''*Which* brother?''

A reminiscent smile tugged at Ross's mouth. "The best-looking one, according to him."

Nancy looked from Travis's disgusted expression to Kara's amusement.

"*Jake,*" they all said in unison.

Ross laughed. "Right. When I called the store looking for you, he answered the phone. Hell of a nice guy, by the way. He said you've dreamed about hosting a fishing guide show for years. That this might be a backdoor in. He hopes your sense of obligation to this place won't prevent you from grabbing a golden career opportunity."

"He said all that, did he?"

"Yeah. Made me wish I had a brother. I love my two sisters, don't get me wrong, but they're not—" Breaking off, Ross tweaked the crease of his khaki slacks self-consciously. "You just be sure and hang on to Jake."

"Oh, I plan to." Resettling his cap, Travis grimly tugged down the bill.

Nancy pictured Jake in a headlock and bit her lip to keep from laughing.

"Anyway, as I was saying, Kara's right about Malloy Sporting Goods," Ross continued. "If the show's a success, an advertising endorsement from you will pack the aisles."

"You said the show's viewing audience would be mostly women. The store's customers are mostly men."

"Right. But women talk to their men about every little detail of their day. They'll find a way to mention the rugged TV hunk that made their hearts go pitter-patter. And—" Ross spoke over Travis's disbelieving huff "—once the ads hit, their husbands and boyfriends will check out the store, hoping some of that testosterone will rub off on them. Don't forget also that women do the majority of Christmas shopping in the family. Your dad's cash registers will be ringing *Jingle Bells* this season."

The thought sent a warm little thrill through Nancy. John worked so hard. And new lines of worry had appeared on his handsome face in recent months. She could see that Travis was mulling over the possibilities of helping his father.

"Didn't I hear Cameron advise John to pump up promotion for the Thanksgiving Sale this year?" she asked casually.

Travis's sour look promised retribution.

Time to retreat and take cover. She scraped back her chair. "Somebody must be as hungry as I am. It's way past the lunch hour. Who wants a ham and Swiss cheese sandwich?"

Kara frowned and looked at her watch.

Both men perked up.

"Sounds great," Travis said appreciatively. "Mustard and tomato only for me. Oh, and some of that potato salad you made last night."

Intercepting Kara's startled glance, Nancy hastened to explain. "Sometimes I'll bring groceries from home and start dinner here. It's no trouble to make extra for Travis, and he does love potato salad."

"*Your* potato salad," he qualified.

She smiled fondly. "You love anything not dumped out of a can or nuked in the microwave. I've never known anyone more useless in a kitchen..." She trailed off, noticing Kara's stiff posture and pink cheeks.

Oh, dear. As a bride, Kara had been all thumbs in the kitchen.

Flustered, Nancy turned to Ross. "What would you like on your sandwich?"

He offered a charming smile. "Mayonnaise, lettuce and tomato...if you're sure it's no trouble?"

"Not at all—"

"Of *course* it's trouble," Kara cut in. "We wouldn't think of imposing. We've got to head back to Houston soon, anyway. Right, Ross?"

His stomach picked that moment to growl loudly.

Everyone laughed. Well, almost everyone.

"Lighten up, Kara," Travis groused. "Not every woman thinks making a simple sandwich is a big deal. Tell Nancy you want mustard, lettuce and tomato but no cheese, say thank you, and let Ross eat, for cripe's sake."

Kara's neutral expression didn't fool Nancy.

If only John hadn't cautioned Travis against reviving a dead relationship! One encouraging word would have smoothed Kara's path. Because she wasn't over Travis, not by a long shot. Nancy recognized the signs intimately.

Rising, she stared hard at the man who'd been kindness personified since her father died. "I swear, Travis, I don't even recognize you today. Keep a civil tongue in your head, or canned chili and frozen dinners is *all* you'll be eating from now on."

His gaze faltered and dropped.

Satisfied, she looked at Kara. "Please do stay for lunch. It's really no bother, and it'll save you from having to stop on the drive home. Besides—" she leaned forward and adopted a conspiratorial tone "—between you, me and Ross, we ought to be able to polish off all Travis's potato salad."

A glint of wry amusement banished the careful blankness in Kara's eyes. "All right, you win. But at least let me help you." She started to rise.

Nancy waved her back down. "Don't be silly. We just bandaged those hands. Tell me what you want on your sandwich."

Shaking her head with a smile, Kara capitulated. "Mustard, lettuce and tomato…but no cheese, thank you."

Travis had gotten it on the nose. Interesting.

"Coming right up," Nancy said, including the others in her smile. "Y'all behave and finish the meeting without me."

As if they needed her, she thought, moving from the breakfast nook into the shabby but spotless kitchen. She was much more at ease putting together lunch than a business deal.

Oh, she could schedule fishing trips, handle correspondence and do light bookkeeping well enough. But she hadn't read the towering stacks of *Time* magazines filling one corner of Travis's office, or the books on business, marketing strategy and a host of other subjects packing his bookcase. She didn't have Kara's MBA degree.

The discussion had lost Nancy with the introduction of macro segmentation. They'd moved on from there to a host's role in stimulating studio audiences, and were now discussing contracts, sounding like a bunch of lawyers.

Shaking her head in wonder, Nancy opened the ancient refrigerator and pulled out the makings for "simple" sandwiches.

Travis's rudeness minutes before had shocked her.

So what if Kara wasn't a whiz in the kitchen? She was smart and interesting and cat-burglar stunning dressed all in black, a perfect foil for her platinum hair and mysterious green eyes. From his mesmerized expression when he looked at Kara, he wasn't over her any more than she was him. Come to think of it, his rudeness was probably an act of self-defense.

Broken hearts took years to mend. No one wanted to experience that kind of pain a second time.

Then again, one didn't always have a choice.

Nancy absently sliced tomatoes, washed lettuce and spread mustard or mayonnaise as ordered, her thoughts drifting back ten years, to when she was thirty-six and weary of dead-end jobs in Dallas. She'd moved back in with her father to help run Larry's Bait Shop about the same time Travis settled into the Malloy family lake house with his new bride....

Nancy liked the demure young woman who was obviously out of her element but deeply in love with her husband. Kara often dropped by the shop to visit during the long hours Travis spent on the lake. Nancy reciprocated when business was slow. They might've become better friends if Kara hadn't begun driving into Houston daily.

And, of course, if Joey Harrison hadn't strutted into Larry's Bait Shop one morning soon after.

Lake Kimberly Marina's newest resident fishing guide was thirty-five, divorced and Viking gorgeous. He'd heard Larry's had a good supply of waterdogs and had come to check it out. He hadn't known the "prettiest woman in Texas" helped run the shop, or he would've come in much much sooner.

Nancy was enthralled.

After an hour of shameless flirting, Joey left with the live bait he wanted and a heart he didn't. Not then, or months later, when he told her so in no uncertain terms. Shortly thereafter, he got caught cheating during a fishing tournament, was subsequently fired from Lake Kimberly Marina's staff, and moved from the area.

She heard that Kara and Travis separated, but was too immersed in her own misery to be much of a friend to the younger woman. Her father's health declined. Her workload increased. She simply had no energy to spare for more than a passing sadness at the news of Kara's divorce.

Four years later, Nancy found her father sprawled on the ground next to the mailbox. She frantically started CPR, but the massive coronary had already taken Larry to that lunker-stocked fishing hole in the sky. He died clutching a warning of forfeiture from the tax assessor collector's office. After five years of evading taxes, his number was finally up.

And Nancy was out of a home.

Her father's funeral was packed. Generations of fishermen to whom he'd given advice and current lake conditions filled the pews. John Malloy and his sons Travis, Seth, Cameron and Jake were among them.

When Travis came forward and offered her a job at Bass Busters Fishing Camp, plus use of one of the cabins until she found a suitable place to live, she cried and thanked him profusely. He said it had been his father's idea.

John Malloy had "seen how hard she worked at the bait shop, how knowledgeable she was about fishing and the lake itself." The job wasn't charity, Travis insisted, it was good business for all concerned.

In returning a portion of her self-respect that day, John had stolen a bit of her heart. After four years and counting, he now possessed it in full.

Too bad his still belonged to a woman who'd been dead for twenty years.

"Nancy?"

She clapped a hand over her chest and looked over her shoulder. "Travis! I didn't see you there."

"Are you okay?"

She forced a bright smile. "You caught me daydreaming."

"Must've been some dream. You've been staring at those for a good while, now." He gestured to the countertop. "Want me to take them to the table?"

Turning, she saw four loaded plates lined up on the beige Formica. She'd piled the potato salad high, sliced the sandwiches and even garnished with pickles. Scary.

"Thank you, that would be a big help. Grab some napkins and forks while you're at it, and I'll pour iced tea for everyone."

She'd just completed filling the last glass when

she heard sneakers on crushed shell near the kitchen door. Her heart lifted joyfully. The door exploded open, slamming against the light blue wall with cringing force.

A sturdy tow-headed boy of eight barreled inside, dropped his backpack and skidded to a comical stop. He looked from the seated strangers to Travis, then quickly to Nancy, who gave him a reassuring smile.

The light of her life was home from school.

"Hey, buddy," Travis said, recapturing the boy's attention. "How many times are you gonna make me patch that wall?"

"Sorry." Ducking his head, Jeremy peeked up through his lashes. "Today's Tuesday."

"I haven't forgotten." Travis looked at Nancy, his expression suddenly as sheepish as the boy's. "He wants to test out his new rod and reel on the lake before dark. I said I'd take him out on my boat—if it's okay with you."

Splaying a hand on one hip, she captured evasive gray eyes. "What about homework, young man?"

"I did it at school already. Honest."

She looked at Travis. "What about Cabin One's leaking faucet?"

"I'll fix it first thing in the morning." He grinned and crossed his chest with an index finger. "I promise."

She heaved an affectionate sigh. Travis was more

of a big brother to Jeremy than a responsible father figure. That role went hands down to John Malloy.

"You kids will cook up anything to get out of doing chores." Meeting Kara's stunned gaze, Nancy arched a brow and pointed. "The short blond one with the missing front tooth is Jeremy Royce. My son."

THE NEXT MORNING Kara unlocked the door of Taylor Fine Foundations, pushed through and turned immediately to bolt herself inside. The precaution was a necessary evil. At 7:00 a.m., none of the other merchants sharing the strip center in east Houston would arrive for at least an hour. The security guard they'd jointly hired wouldn't start duty until nine. No sense inviting trouble.

She had enough of that already, thank you.

Sighing, she flipped on the lights and wove past round racks and shelves of serviceable undergarments, the mainstay of Taylor Fine Foundations since 1919. She could recite the store's history as well as most people could the story of "Little Red Riding Hood," having heard the tale early in her life from her grandparents, then filling in gaps later with her own research.

Fresh from World War I, Thomas Taylor had opened his store in the heart of downtown Houston and liberated the city's women from whalebone forever. His first customers lived during a time when the ideal feminine figure was modeled upon a boyish shape.

Since few women were actually shaped like boys, Taylor Fine Foundations was there to help them achieve slim androgynous silhouettes. Then, and also fifty years later.

Women weren't shaped like Twiggy, either.

Yep, Kara had to hand it to her ancestor. He'd been one shrewd cookie, capitalizing on the truism he'd borrowed from fashion designer Christian Dior. She entered the back office and flipped the light switch next to the framed autographed photo of the designer.

"Without foundations, there can be no fashion," Kara quoted aloud, then headed straight for the coffeemaker on top of a dented file cabinet. Within minutes, she leaned against the wall waiting for that first blissful cup.

In preparation for taking over the family business, she'd become something of a lingerie history buff. New technology, man-made textiles, and her gender's slavery to fashion and the entertainment industry had all impacted undergarments dramatically.

You could trace the progression of women's emancipation by studying underwear. The correlation had fascinated her in college. It still did.

Now when she flipped through Gram's treasured family photo album, Kara envisioned the foundations under the fashions. And the lives each woman led.

Great-grandmother Letty, so daring in her straight "short" flapper dress. No doubt wearing a corselette utilizing new two-way-stretch elastic panels, rebelling against a return to prewar dependence by minimizing her womanly curves and emulating the freedom of men.

Posing fifteen years later on the portico of Taylor House, great-aunt Emma, elegant in a belted slim-skirted day dress. The Sleekie corselette underneath, developed for Hollywood actresses to prevent rustling in talkies, gave her the confidence of Greta Garbo and Marlene Dietrich.

One of Kara's favorite photos featured Gram in the fifties, decked out for a night of dancing at the Shamrock Club. Her strapless dress, tightly belted with a full skirt worn over crinoline petticoats, depended on a "torsolette" to cinch her waist and plump her breasts. By then, the application of DuPont's nylon patent manipulated women's bodies into overtly sexy shapes.

When Kara had first teased Gram about looking like Marilyn Monroe, she'd said, "It was the fashion. Besides, a lady is as a lady does."

Sighing, Kara straightened from the wall and poured herself a mug of steaming coffee. In her grandmother's eyes, modeling for a lingerie catalog was a Grand Canyon leap from fashionable to inexpressibly tacky.

Desperate measures, she reminded herself grimly.

Carrying her mug to Thomas's original Stowe Davis desk, she sat in his son Douglas's leather executive chair and eyed the shabby office sadly.

At the height of Houston's oil-boom days in the seventies, her grandfather had overseen a chain of twenty-five stores. The devastating oil bust of the next decade had whittled the number to five by the year he died.

Gram had assumed control of the stores, insisting that Kara finish graduate school, and later, be a helpmate to her new husband. By the time Kara woke up and realized her grandmother was struggling—and failing—to run the business efficiently, two more stores had shut down.

Kara had begun driving daily into Houston, the beginning of the end to her marriage. Although Travis loved Gram, he resented Kara arriving home at eight o'clock—despite the fact he was often gone himself, the hypocrite. The separation and divorce had at least saved her that wearing drive.

With no hands-on experience, a wounded heart and no capital to remodel or modernize image through aggressive advertising, she'd nonetheless held onto the remaining three stores. Consolidating everything last year into this final location had been voluntary. A seasoned retail warrior's strongest defense against the inevitable.

Custer's last stand.

Frowning, Kara leaned forward and switched on her computer, an ancient model that took forever to boot up, then grabbed her coffee on the way back. She was tired of negative thoughts. For the first time in many months, there was a faint light at the end of the tunnel.

Travis had agreed to co-host the pilot!

If KLUV-TV's program director liked the results, she and Travis were guaranteed a hefty advance sum to tape eight more shows.

If—no, *when*—the pilot went well, she would pay her most delinquent due bills and the staggering postal costs of a city-wide catalog mailing. She would pump the profits into new cash registers, carpet and dressing rooms for the store. She would keep the business alive for another year. For Gram.

Suddenly Travis's voice resounded in Kara's head, taunting and painful: *"You're the one who'd be crushed if the last store closes. 'Cause that would mean you couldn't cut it as a wife or a businesswoman."*

The shrill ring of the phone pierced her thoughts.

Kara jerked, sending coffee sloshing over her hand and onto the desk. "Rats!"

She searched for something to use as a blotter to

prevent a coffee waterfall onto her lap. Good thing the liquid had missed her keyboard.

The phone rang again.

"I'm coming," she muttered, snatching up a pair of high-waist cotton panties from a sample box near her feet. Ugly thing, but wonderfully absorbent.

Still dabbing, she answered on the third ring. "Taylor Fine Foundations."

"Oh, good, you're there. So tell me everything," Lisa demanded.

CHAPTER SEVEN

"GOOD MORNING to you, too," Kara said dryly.

"I've got an early tennis game. No time for politeness." Lisa slurped something loudly.

"Obviously not. I thought you kicked the Diet Coke habit."

A beat of guilty silence. "Mother's been on my case again about Chad. It was either fall off the wagon, or drive it right down her throat."

Mrs. Williams lobbied periodically for Lisa to marry the next probable partner of her father's prestigious law firm. A presentable and handy escort for the many social functions she attended. And, according to Lisa, too in love with himself to spare any for her.

Kara made a sound of sympathy. "How many proposals does this make, now?"

"Three. I swear Mother's got him convinced he won't make partner until I say 'yes.' Anyway, enough about that." Another slurp. "I've been *dying* to know what happened yesterday. Did you convince Travis to do the show?"

"Yes." Kara extended the receiver a safe distance from her ear, grinning at the audible whoop. When it faded, she snugged the phone back into place. "I had to do some fancy tap dancing, though. He's not exactly motivated to help me. But he always did love Gram."

"Who wouldn't? But don't fool yourself, hon. I watched Major McKinney's video tape. With the sparks flying across that auditorium, Vanessa Allen could've been chopped liver for all anybody cared. It's obvious there's a lot of strong feeling left between you and Travis."

"Yeah. It's called hate."

"Tell that to someone who didn't watch you cry yourself sick those first months of your separation."

The coffee in Kara's stomach roiled.

"Besides, you know what they say about the fine line between love and hate."

"Don't go there, Lisa. I really can't deal with it now, okay?"

"Well...sure, Kara. Hey, I'm sorry."

Thank goodness.

"It's just that since bumping into Travis again you've seemed more...I don't know, animated. I can't help wishing that the two of you would—"

"Ross asked about you on the drive back to Houston."

After a telling pause, Lisa said with studied casualness, "Oh?"

"Yes, he did." Kara let the silence stretch.

"You're going to make me beg for it, aren't you?"

"I should."

"I *said* I was sorry."

True. "You promise to keep your wishful thinking to yourself?"

"Girl Scout's honor."

"You never made it past Brownies." Lisa had decided the green Girl Scout uniform made her look sallow and had dropped out.

"All-right-all-right, I *promise*. Satisfied?"

Now that her friend was thoroughly distracted, Kara relented. "Ross asked if you were involved with anyone. So I told him about Chad."

"Kara!"

She'd forgotten how much fun teasing could be. "Calm down. I told him you were available. But I'd watch my step if I were you. I mean, it's not that I don't like him, but I get the impression he enjoys playing the field. He's pretty much married to his job."

Kara spent the next ten minutes listening to denials of any serious interest in Ross. Lisa was smitten all right. And with a man who actually might not jump through her hoops.

Slurp. "Oh—before I forget. Have you told Vinnie yet that he can forget meeting the Mystery Woman?"

Rats. "I called him, yes." During the heavy silence, she pictured dark eyes narrowing. "Hey, don't you have a tennis game waiting?"

"Unbelievable, Taylor. When is he flying in?"

Ah, well. "We didn't confirm the calendar date, only the 'date' date. I'll try to hold him off as long as I can, since things will be pretty crazy before the first taping." Understatement of the year.

"You're out of your mind, you know. It'll take a miracle for him not to discover the truth...."

Kara twirled the phone cord glumly.

"...or a more devious mind than yours. How can I help?"

A flood of emotion made speaking difficult. "I'll let you know. And Lisa...?" She brought the cord to her chest and pressed hard.

"You're welcome," Lisa said gently. "Don't get maudlin on me." She cleared her throat. "Gotta run now and justify choosing tennis over piano lessons. Keep me posted. Buh-bye."

"Bye," Kara managed, smiling mistily as she hung up.

Leaning back in her chair, she pressed her fingertips together and thanked God for sending her Lisa. Through thick and thin, for better and for worse, she'd been a constant and faithful friend.

She'd helped Kara get through an ugly duckling stage lasting into her late teens. A heady but frightening flurry of male attention in college. A whirlwind courtship with Travis, and subsequent marriage, separation and divorce. A battle to keep Taylor Fine Foundations alive. And more boxes of tissues and bags of Oreos than she cared to admit to.

Resigning herself to life without Travis had been hard, but Kara honestly didn't know if she could survive without her best friend.

Maybe if her mother had lived…no, even if Pamela Taylor were alive, she wouldn't offer the support Kara got from Lisa.

Kara had learned the full grim truth about her mother only after taking over the family business, when Carol had begun dropping thinly veiled hints. Pressed for details, she'd feigned reluctance to betray Gram's trust. But she'd spilled the beans soon enough.

Apparently Pamela had spent half her life in and out of jail and drug rehabilitation programs, using Taylor House as a pit stop in between. One day, she'd dropped four-year-old Kara off to visit Douglas and Esther, and had never bothered to return. Six months later, she'd died of a drug overdose.

Gram still maintained the pretense that Pamela had been a wonderful person and daughter, her death the result of a car accident while driving to Dallas.

But now Kara understood so much. Why her grandparents had preached the importance of holding her head up, being a lady, never showing the world weakness, doing the Taylor name proud. Why she'd sensed them watching her like a time bomb as she grew. Why pleasing them, and later others, had defined her worth.

Why failure was intolerable.

Disgusted, Kara rose and headed for the coffee machine for a refill. Enough negative thoughts. She wouldn't fail. But she'd better take care of her private business fast. Carol was due to work in about twenty minutes, and the woman had eyes in the back of her head.

Kara returned to her desk, scooted her chair closer to the computer keyboard and accessed her e-mail. Opening the daily report from her fulfillment house was the highlight of each morning. Ah, good. Orders from the last *Mystery Woman* mailing were still trickling in. Twelve had been received the day before.

The corselette with lace and satin ribbon trim was a definite winner. Life was funny. Her great-grandfather had established his success by introducing the same garment.

Kara's version used a mixture of nylon and Lycra rather than "loomed elastic," and it enhanced rather than compressed a woman's natural shape, but the trend back to more complex—and therefore mysterious to the opposite sex—lingerie was one she wouldn't ignore.

Making a mental note to photograph it in red for

the Christmas and Valentine's Day mania ahead, she cleared out her other mail, typed in an address on the Internet and hit go.

Lord, wouldn't Travis be shocked at her catalog venture? Although…he had appeared to look at her differently the day before. As if he'd seen her in a new light.

Her. The real Kara Taylor.

Not a genteel Southern flower whose main joy in life was to make a home for her man. Or a spoiled hothouse flower, the term he'd used when she'd rebelled against the role he expected her to love.

That he hadn't quite known what to make of the real her was fine and dandy. He'd thrown a few curves her way, too.

Sipping her coffee, she stared at her monitor wide-eyed. The home page for Bass Busters Fishing Camp was slick, professional and very state of the art. This from a man who'd balked at adding bathrooms to the cabins, arguing that community showers and toilets were fine for serious fishermen. And that he "wasn't running a resort."

Maybe not, but he sure emphasized private bathrooms now on his list of amenities.

She scanned his list of published articles, including, "Five Deadly Strategies To Attack Lunker Bass," "Retrieves That Make Jerkbaits Come Alive," "Top Ten Underfished Big Bass Lakes." Scintillating stuff.

Ten minutes later, Kara relaxed back in her chair, dazed and impressed in spite of herself. Well.

The camp might not have changed much in nine years, but Travis had indeed become a recognized master in the sport of bass fishing. What's more, his writing skill matched the verbal prowess that had always won him arguments in their marriage. In addition to articles in *Field and Stream*, *In-Fisherman* and *Advanced Fishing Strategies*, he wrote a monthly on-line newsletter. She never would've guessed he was so versatile.

But then, apparently she'd been oblivious to a lot of things about the people around her when she'd left Lake Kimberly. Like Nancy's pregnancy.

Nancy had a son! Kara still couldn't get over the news. It filled her with guilt for neglecting to keep in touch with her friend, as well as more than a trace of biological-time-clock envy.

Jeremy Royce was the image of Joey Harrison. But the boy had looked at Travis with the love most children would feel for their father. Or so Kara imagined. Regardless of any other faults she might attribute to her ex-husband, she'd never doubted he would make a terrific dad…

I figure when the time is right, we can convert one of the cabins into our office and make the second bedroom a nursery. Put a little blond-haired green-eyed angel in the crib.

Kara's heart constricted. Torturing herself with

what might have been was so pointless and self-indulgent. How much worse it must be for Nancy, who lived with the knowledge that Jeremy's father wanted nothing to do with either of them!

Nancy had pulled Kara aside before she'd left and explained Joey's abandonment with quiet dignity. Jeremy had been told a softened version of the truth only this year, and had never asked questions about his father again. An all-too-common situation in modern life. So infuriating.

So very sad.

Shutting down her computer, Kara nursed her coffee and heartfelt empathy. The biggest victim in all this, of course, was the innocent child. Jeremy would wonder, even after growing up, why his father hadn't loved him enough to be a part of his life.

Perhaps when he reached adulthood, he would track Joey down and ask. That's what she would've done, given the same chance.

Kara swallowed the last of her coffee audibly.

Though Gram had fabricated a false image for her daughter, she'd stopped short of inventing a son-in-law. Pamela had not only never wed, she'd also never revealed who'd fathered her child.

Unfortunately, Kara's question would always remain unanswered.

TRAVIS STEERED his Jeep next to the curb in front of Taylor House, parked behind two cars and assessed the situation. Kara's blue Toyota sat in the driveway. The silver Mercedes belonged to Ross. Travis didn't know who owned the little red Miata convertible. Apparently someone else was joining them.

Good.

'Cause he sure wasn't gonna be much help.

Three days ago at the camp, Ross had suggested they all have a brainstorming session to nail down a name for the show. They "should meet someplace comfortable and private," so that meant the TV station was out. Travis had said his kitchen table worked fine for him—and been pretty much ignored for his trouble.

Then, giving Kara a funny look, Ross had wondered aloud if her grandmother might like to sit in on the session at, say, Taylor House. The way Kara had lit up like silver jerkbait in murky water, you'd have thought the producer was brilliant.

Too lazy to drive was more like it.

Travis had left in plenty of time to be here at two o'clock, but a wreck had slowed traffic to a crawl. Now he was thirty minutes late for a meeting that was plain silly.

Why couldn't the man just pick a name? Any name. No one was going to watch the stupid show anyway.

Opening the Jeep door, Travis swung his legs to

the street, pulled up one limp tube sock, retied the laces to his Nike cross trainers and yanked down the hem of his jeans.

Okay, he could do this. He hadn't seen or talked to Esther since things went sour with Kara, and the thought of that sweet woman's censure made his palms sweat. But procrastinating wouldn't help.

He was as presentable as he was going to get.

Standing, he was suddenly glad he'd changed at the last minute from his worn blue plaid flannel shirt into this hunter-green corduroy job. It was in decent shape, except for a tiny hole in the collar way in back, where his hair covered the evidence. Two years ago, Nancy had *said* Jeremy was too young to cast safely, and she'd been right. Not that Travis had told her so.

Hell, she would've ripped into him worse than any miscast hook.

Slamming the Jeep door, he pocketed his keys and stared in dismay at the two-story home he'd loved to visit. Built by famed architect John Staub, Taylor House had once been the crown jewel of this old neighborhood. Not any more.

The flower beds along the left fence line were choked with weeds, the rose bushes spindly and sparsely blooming. The sprawling live oak on the right looked as if several large limbs had broken off. Handiwork of the hurricane in late August,

probably. Damn shame. That tree had to be close
to a hundred years old.

The four fluted columns supporting the roofed
front porch were dingy gray now rather than dazzling white. A peeling black shutter flanking one of
the upstairs windows sagged drunkenly. The roof
had lost a good third of its shingles. Four window
screens were missing.

Travis felt a little sick.

He walked slowly toward the portico, noting the
rusting black wrought-iron chairs that needed sand-
ing, priming and repainting, the "white" planked
wood floor that needed the same. His conversation
with Kara in the boat shed replayed in his mind.

*It's not the store closing that I'm most worried
about. Unless cash flow improves, I'll have to sell
Taylor House and everything inside it.*

Are things really that bad?

Yes, Travis, they're that bad.

At the time, he'd remembered how she'd given
up on their marriage after one measly year and
hightailed it back to save Taylor Fine Foundations
instead. Faced now with the tangible proof of her
reduced financial circumstances, he was more
ashamed than ever of his initial spurt of triumph.

She'd actually tripped in her haste to get away
from his mean-spiritedness!

Releasing a disgusted breath now, Travis reached
the front door and stopped. He'd been a real jerk,

all right. Maybe he couldn't change history, or his residual feelings of hurt, but he could do his level best to get through the next few weeks without sending Kara running.

He lifted the tarnished brass knocker and rapped twice.

Silence. Seconds later, light footsteps sounded on the marble foyer.

"Travis, dear, is that you?" a voice warbled from the other side of the door, the tone warm and welcoming.

Travis's frown melted, along with his heart. He'd been fourteen when his mother died. The edges of his memories were blurred, but she'd called him "dear," too. She'd been gracious and kind. An impeccable lady, like Esther Taylor.

"It's me, beautiful," Travis confirmed. "Now open up and give me a hug."

The dead bolt unlatched and the door swung inward.

Travis swooped forward and lifted Esther in a twirling hug, smiling against her Brillo pad hair. She trilled girlishly, but he noted how thin and frail she felt, as if a hard squeeze would crush her bones. Stopping, he set her gently on her feet.

"My goodness!" Flushed, her pale blue eyes sparkling, she shut the door and turned back to face him, patting her undisturbed blue-gray curls. "I must look a fright."

In neat black slacks and a pink tunic sweater, her carefully applied lipstick a perfect match, she appeared youthful and coquettish.

He grinned. "You look younger and even more gorgeous than you did nine years ago. What's your secret, Esther?"

"Compliments from handsome young devils." She pushed his arm playfully. "Just look at you! I do believe you've gotten bigger. Is that possible?"

He made a rueful face and patted his stomach. "Time to cut back on the potato salad."

"Nonsense. There's not an ounce of fat on you."

Again, he glimpsed the beautiful Southern flirt who must've kept a host of beaus dangling before Douglas Taylor severed the marionette strings.

Travis leaned down, kissed her papery cheek and murmured in her ear, "I've missed you, Esther."

"And I've missed you, dear. It's been far too long."

Pulling away, she grasped his hands and squeezed. They exchanged a sappy little smile.

A masculine throat cleared loudly, interrupting the moment. Travis looked toward the source.

The tall elderly man watching beside Kara from the living room entryway stood ramrod straight, his alert dark eyes a striking contrast to his short silver hair. Suddenly glad he'd been gentle with Esther, Travis turned his attention to Kara.

She was giving him *That Look*.

Soft and wondering, as if he'd done something special. As a graduate student, Kara had looked at him like that after he'd dispensed with the creep pawing her at Seth's fraternity house party.

Travis had fallen hard for That Look.

From then on, he'd worked to inspire it often, and had even succeeded—until about six months after their wedding, when disappointment had begun dimming the glow in her eyes.

She appeared to collect herself and assumed an expression matching her no-nonsense gray jacket and skirt. "Ross has been here for thirty minutes. We really should get started."

He blinked. "Sure. Sorry I'm late. There was a four-car accident on I-45. Only one lane was moving."

"How horrible!" Esther exclaimed, hooking her arm through his and walking with him toward her granddaughter. "The Interstate scares me to death. I used to worry so when Kara commuted from Lake Kimberly to Houston every day."

So had he.

"It must be even more dangerous now, with residential development spreading north, and more cars than ever using the freeway." Esther pulled him to a stop. "I do hope you'll be careful on the drive home, Travis."

"Gram, please! The man just got here. Let him sit down before you start picturing him in an am-

bulance.'' Frowning, she met his eyes. ''It's a good
thing you showed up. She was ready to call the
hospitals at two-fifteen. Major McKinney convinced her to wait until three, but not even he
could've stopped her after that.''

''O-oh, don't you listen to her, Travis. I wouldn't
have called until at *least* three-fifteen.''

Although everyone laughed, including Kara, her
underlying annoyance puzzled Travis. So, Esther
worried? Her daughter had been killed in a car accident, for cripe's sake.

''Travis, dear, I'd like you to meet a good friend
we invited to help us brainstorm. I must admit I
was a little nervous about coming up with ideas,
and thought reinforcements would be wise.''

Kara spoke up. ''None of us have done this before. There's no need to be nervous. We're all in
the same boat.''

Esther's shrewd gaze locked with her granddaughter's. ''It does appear that way, doesn't it?
Although I wish you would reconsider and tell that
nice Mr. Hadley he'll need to find another hostess
for the show.''

''We've been through all this, Gram. Remember
your manners. Shouldn't you finish the introduction?''

Esther started, then grew pink. ''Goodness, forgive me, Travis. This is Major Wayne McKinney.
He retired from the army and moved next door after

you and Kara…well, about six years ago. Wayne, meet Travis Malloy.''

Travis exchanged a firm solid handshake that revealed the older man's vigor and directness. ''A pleasure, Major McKinney.''

''Likewise. Esther's told me a lot about you.'' His keen brown eyes seemed to know that Travis was wondering what the hell she'd said.

The Major didn't elaborate.

''O-oh, don't mind him.'' Esther glanced reprovingly at her neighbor. ''I told him you were a fine young man, and that I was sorry you and Kara couldn't…that you two got…''

''*Divorced*, Gram. You can say it out loud. It's not a bad word, you know.'' Kara turned and huffed off into the living room.

Major McKinney shrugged sympathetically at Esther, then followed.

From Esther's strained expression, Travis assumed this was a familiar sore subject. He'd never considered Kara might've gotten as much grief from her grandmother about the divorce as he had from his father and brothers.

Esther glanced at him hesitantly. ''I hope I didn't offend you.''

Travis laughed. ''If you knew my brothers better, you wouldn't need to ask.''

''I can hardly believe that. Such fine polite boys

they were. And so handsome!'' Esther's expression grew wistful. ''They must be all grown up now.''

The ''boys'' had been eighteen, twenty and twenty-two when she had met them, but Travis empathized more than he'd like with Esther. Hell, the older he got, the younger everybody else seemed.

She recovered her gracious smile. ''And how's your dear father?''

Lonely.

The thought came out of nowhere, imbued with the strength of truth. He nudged it aside to examine later. ''Working too hard, but otherwise doing fine. You know, maybe we'd better get in there—'' he nodded toward the living room ''—before the natives get too restless. Shall we?''

He brought his opposite hand over to cover the fragile fingers placed on his arm, and escorted Esther through the double doors.

Instantly his stomach tensed.

He'd always felt big and awkward in this room of fancy geegaws, lace doilies and furniture that creaked when you sat. Everything was old. Not the comfortable kind of old, where you didn't worry about knocking over lamps or spilling drinks, but the antique kind, where Tiffany glass shades and oriental rugs were irreplaceable heirlooms.

Above the fireplace hung a framed black-and-white photograph of Esther and Douglas in formal wedding attire. They looked stiff, happy, and as perfect together as figurines topping a three-tiered wedding cake.

Ross and Major McKinney stood in front of two olive-green wing-back chairs that rounded out a seating area in front of the fireplace. Kara sat rigidly on a camelback wine-red sofa. Opposite her, a small dark-haired woman watched Ross from a matching love seat.

"Actually, divorce isn't a bad word," the producer was saying. He held up a finger. "Now alimony—*that's* offensive. Just ask my CPA."

Chuckles broke out, and the strain eased. The petite brunette turned and met his gaze.

Recognition hit.

He'd only been around her a few times, but she wasn't the kind of female a man forgot. Dressed in a clingy short sweater dress the color of her ivory skin, her luminous dark eyes the same shade as her hair, she was still a knockout.

But if she was also still fiercely protective of her best friend, his ex-wife, he could be in for a bumpy ride.

"Hello, Lisa," he said warily. "Good to see you again."

CHAPTER EIGHT

"GOOD TO SEE YOU, TOO, Travis." Lisa studied him
with frank curiosity, then added a warm smile for
Esther. "Come sit by me, Gram. There's plenty of
room."

"Thank you, Lisa. That would be lovely."

Travis led Esther forward and helped her lower
stiffly onto the love seat. While leaning over, he
glanced above blue-gray curls and caught Lisa staring. At his butt.

Instead of blushing, she offered a so-sue-me
shrug and flashed irresistible dimples. Apparently
she had no hard feelings.

He straightened from his task and grinned. "I see
they roped you into this brainstorming thing, too."

"No. I invited myself when Kara mentioned it.
I'm here to represent women under thirty, which I
can still do for three more months. Unlike *some* of
us, who are thirty going on old-fogy."

A feminine snort sounded from the sofa. "Better
that than twenty-nine going on teenybopper."

"Kara," Esther chided gently. "We have guests,

remember? Travis, do make yourself comfortable, dear.''

Comfortable?

Ensconced firmly in their man-size chairs, Ross and the Major avoided his eyes. Travis moved reluctantly to the sofa and sat.

Sure enough his rump barely fit, his knees poked out to Lake Kimberly, and his submarine Nikes went aground on the oriental rug. Trying to remember if he'd wiped his feet on the welcome mat, he grew aware of the unnatural quiet.

The men smirked at each other, Esther watched him with affectionate amusement and Lisa appeared fascinated with his feet. God only knew what expression Kara wore. Travis wasn't about to turn and find out.

His neck burning, he blurted, ''So, Lisa? That must be your new Miata parked in front. How does it handle?''

Her startled gaze rose and warmed. ''Like a dream! I've really enjoyed driving it.''

''Yeah, and if you're really nice to her,'' Kara added, ''maybe she'll give you a ride to the mall later.''

Supremely indifferent, Lisa examined her crimson manicure. ''Sticks and stones.''

Travis smothered a grin. ''Looks like a fun car to me.''

Lisa's apathy vanished. She recrossed her legs and sent him a dazzling smile. "*Thank* you, it is."

Ross loosened his necktie with an irritable motion. "Pretty impractical. It's too hot in Houston to drive a convertible."

Following the direction of his gaze, Travis felt a kindred sympathy. Kara's skirt wasn't as short as her friend's, but her legs were just as shapely. And longer. Much much longer. Plus, he knew her habit of wearing lingerie that dried a man's mouth as fast as he could drool.

Damn. Travis hooked a finger over his collar and pulled.

"You sound as bad as Kara," Lisa told Ross. "The weather's been perfect this week. I keep trying to get her to drive around town with me, but she won't even get inside."

"Correction," Kara interjected. "I *can't* get inside. And even if I could, can you imagine the picture we'd make? You...tucked low behind the wheel—not to mention windshield—looking sporty and sexy. Me...towering like Gulliver traveling beside you, bugs smashing into my face. Thanks, but no thanks."

Lisa laughed. "Do you hear how ridiculous you sound?"

Esther frowned sweetly. "I wish you wouldn't refer to yourself in such a derogatory manner, Kara. A tall woman has such grace, such presence."

"So does Michael Jordan. But we'd both look silly in a Miata, and nobody would rush to help us get in or out of the thing the way they would you or Lisa. I hate to sound sexist, but for a woman, being dainty is definitely better than having 'presence.' Dainty is feminine. Dainty is *power.*"

Lisa reached over and patted Esther's knee. "You can't win this one, Gram. I've tried since elementary school, when Sister Regina picked Kara to be Joseph in the nativity play because she was the tallest."

"No shame in that," Major McKinney declared staunchly. "I played a girl once in a production of *South Pacific* at Anderson Military Academy."

Kara flashed a rueful smile. "I appreciate your gallantry, Major, but St. Francis Parochial School was coed. Since I was taller than all the boys, and since Sister Regina wanted a Joseph with *presence*—" she shot her grandmother a pointed look "—I got stuck with the part."

Esther looked distressed. "But Douglas and I were so proud you were selected. We thought you wanted to play Joseph."

"I wanted to be a sheep so I could wear a cute costume made out of cotton balls. But Sister Regina said I would stick out too much and mess up the 'symmetry' of her scene."

Despite her joking tone, Kara's story smacked of a painful childhood memory. The kind a wife would share with her husband, if no one else. Travis wondered uneasily why she hadn't told him.

"Oh, dear." Esther's hand fluttered to her throat. "Why didn't you tell me?"

Kara smoothed her skirt, then lifted a shoulder. "You were proud. If I'd told you the real reason I got picked, you would've felt sorry for me."

"I don't know," Travis found himself saying. "Seems to me like Joseph has a lot more *power* in the nativity scene than a sheep."

After a startled second, genuine amusement curved her mouth. "Nice try, but next to the baby Jesus, Mary had all the power. And I'll give you three guesses who got chosen for *that* part."

Every eye in the room turned to Lisa.

"He-ey. It's not my fault."

"To rub salt in the wound," Kara continued, "Lisa's plastic Thumbelina doll got the part of baby Jesus."

Travis barked a laugh. "I'm afraid to ask, but did a doll of yours audition?"

She nodded, her eyes alight with captivating mischief. "My antique china doll with the beautiful painted face. Sister Regina said it was too 'big' for the cradle."

As sympathetic groans and chuckles broke out, Lisa raised her palms defensively. "See? *This* is what happens to dainty people. They get picked on. Help me out here, Gram."

"I don't mean to be rude," Ross broke in, his tone sobering the group. He reached into his coat pocket and withdrew a small notepad and slim gold pen. "But I've got to meet with the composer and graphic designer tomorrow morning, and so far we've got a great concept for the talk show, but no great name. Somebody want to help *me* out here, please?"

Kara tugged down her jacket with a purposeful air. "You're right, Ross. I'm sorry for getting us sidetracked. We're ready to get serious, now."

"Great. Everybody here know what our goal is?" Ross asked Kara.

"I've already told Lisa and Major McKinney we're looking for a title that's catchy and descriptive of what Travis and I will be doing—rather than using our names. So I'll toss something in the ring now. What does everyone think of 'Double Talk' for a title?"

"Hmm. Not bad." Ross scribbled her suggestion on his pad. "Maybe a little too ambiguous. Let's go with the word 'talk' for a minute. Pillow Talk, Coffee Talk, Baby Talk, Small Talk…"

"Happy Talk?" the Major offered. "Like the song from *South Pacific*. Or…what about Peace Talk?"

"Good!" Ross jotted the second name down. "That's definitely the right direction."

"Very clever, Wayne," Esther praised, causing his face to redden and his chest to expand.

Lisa tapped her chin in concentration. "How about Can We Talk? Everyone knows that famous Joan Rivers line, and women would sure relate to asking the men in their lives that question."

"Write that down, Ross," Kara ordered. "It's good."

He obeyed, his free hand signaling them with a circular motion to keep going.

Esther jumped in. "Talk Big, Talk Mean, Talk Dirty—"

"Gram!" Kara said, laughing.

"What?" Esther blinked innocently, but a twinkle lurked in her eyes. "I'm brainstorming, dear. You can't censor creative flow. Now, where was I? Oh, yes. Talk of the Town, Talk It Over, Talk To Me, Talk About Not Communicating, Tell Me Everything—Tell *Us* Everything, Tell Us More, Tell Us About It, Tell Us Your Version, Speak Up, Speak Out, Speak Our Language, Speak the Same Language, Speak…Speak…give me a second."

Ross scribbled madly while she held up a warning finger.

Esther's brow smoothed. Her finger came down. "Explain It To Us, Explain Yourself, Explain What You Mean, What Do You *Really* Mean?, What Did You Really Say?, You Don't Say?…You Don't Mean It, You…You…"

Travis shared a gaping look with the others.

Esther shrugged apologetically. "Oh, dear. I seem to have run dry for the moment."

Lisa recovered first and raised her hands to her mouth to make a megaphone. "Hear ye, hear ye!" she trumpeted. "I proclaim Esther Taylor the Queen of Brainstorming!"

"Gram, that was unbelievable," Kara seconded. "Did you get that all down, Ross?"

The producer's answer faded into the background as an idea took hold of Travis. He tested the unusual title in his mind, thinking that it met the criteria. Catchy. A good description of what would take place during a show where men and women took turns describing their understanding of a shared event in their relationship.

But hell, what did he know?

"Travis."

He jerked into awareness. "Huh?"

From Kara's expression, it wasn't the first time she'd called his name. "Brother, where have you been? We've narrowed our favorite titles down to 'Peace Talk' and 'Tell Us About It.' Which one gets your vote?"

He drew his feet close to the sofa and gripped his knees. "Um...I'd have to say 'Tell Us About It'—no offense, Major."

"None taken, son. That's my favorite, too. Well, done, Esther."

Lisa chimed in with similar praise. Kara looked at Travis oddly.

Watching Esther pat her hair, blush and wave off their comments with obvious pleasure, Travis made his decision. "Way to go, Esther. Beauty and brains all in one. So, Ross? Looks like we've got our title."

The producer flipped his notebook shut and beamed in satisfaction. "Looks that way—"

"Wait a second," Kara interrupted. She leveled her perceptive green gaze at Travis. "You had an idea just now for a title you didn't share. Throw it out on the table."

Good Lord! Was she psychic? "Esther's is better."

"Oh, do tell us, Travis," Esther pleaded. "I'll feel terrible if you don't."

Thanks a lot, Kara, he told her silently.

Her calm gaze never wavered.

"Well—" Travis stopped and cleared his throat. "I thought of something earlier when Lisa said 'hear ye, hear ye.' Sort of a take on that. You know how the show will be based on hearing men and women speak one at a time? Well, the title 'Hear He, Hear She' came to mind."

No one spoke.

"Stupid idea," he plowed on, his face heating. "I told you Esther's was better."

"Hmm…" Ross muttered the name under his

breath several times, then broke into a smile. "It's brilliant! I love it! We can use trumpet fanfares in the opening music."

Lisa, Esther and the Major began talking at once, endorsing the title enthusiastically. Dazed, Travis met Kara's smiling eyes.

You're welcome, she told him silently.

His chest burned with a familiar—and frightening—warmth. When someone called her name and she looked away, he gave himself a mental lecture.

They would be seeing a lot of each other in the next few weeks. He'd simply have to resist falling under her spell. He could do that. After all, he knew what kind of woman she really was.

But as his fear gradually increased instead of vice versa, he wondered if he really knew Kara at all.

THE NEXT DAY Ross woke at his usual time of five-thirty, then realized he could go back to sleep. He didn't, of course. He lay there without purpose or enthusiasm wondering how he would spend his Saturday. Finally, he got up, made a pot of coffee and turned on the television to fill the silence.

When the newspaper thudded onto his welcome mat, he sighed in relief. That would kill at least an hour. He opened his apartment door to perfect golfing weather...or convertible weather, according to Lisa Williams.

Damn. Why did she keep popping into his head?

Shaking off the distraction, he walked to the sofa and settled comfortably. No golf this weekend. His regular buddies were tied up with family obligations. He didn't want to hook up with strangers for eighteen holes. Ah, well.

Ross snapped open the newspaper, content for the next hour. Then he made eggs and toast, ate slowly, and cleaned his small mess. Now what? His apartment, merely a rest stop between work hours, had never seemed so unappealing.

Probably the contrast with Taylor House, his logic told him. Its antique heirloom furniture, faded Persian area rugs, family photographs and treasured knickknacks made his apartment seem even more cheerless and impersonal than usual. Then, too, Taylor House had Esther, who'd made him feel more welcome, relaxed and "at home" than he had since moving to Houston.

Unable to tolerate moping inside any longer, he decided to take Esther up on her standing invitation "to drop by any time."

Twenty minutes later, when he drove up to the house and saw Lisa's lipstick-red Miata at the curb, his pulse accelerated to warp speed. More than a little disturbed, he parked and sat gripping the wheel, analyzing his reaction.

Kara had once told Ross he didn't want or need her approval. That he knew he was handsome and didn't care what she thought of his character, else

he wouldn't have persisted in trying to get her to
co-host the show after she'd already declined. At
the time, he'd been impressed with her perception.

He liked women. Most women liked him back.

He appreciated their companionship in bed and
out.

But he didn't *need* them. The thought of seeing
a particular woman had never made his heart pound
as hard as it did those first moments before glimps-
ing the latest Nielsen ratings.

Until now.

God, this wasn't part of his Plan.

In new emotional territory, he locked his car and
approached the front door cautiously. Despite repeated knocks and rings, no one answered. Could
they all have gone somewhere in Kara's car?

He walked up the buckled concrete driveway to
the garage, then peered through a side-door win-
dowpane. Empty. Disappointed and loathe to drive
off, he looked speculatively at the weathered cedar
fence enclosing the backyard. The gate beckoned
ten feet away.

He'd snooped this far. Why not go the whole
nosy nine yards? Slipping through the rickety gate,
he could only hope Major McKinney wasn't spying
from behind a curtained window next door.

Inside the backyard, Ross stood a moment to get
his bearings. Someone had obviously been an avid
rose gardener once upon a time. Unkempt beds and

bushes lined the fence, with more edging the small flagstone patio. Four towering oaks dominated the yard, their outspread branches intertwined. Beneath one, a hammock swayed gently on a metal support frame.

The surge of Ross's heart confirmed his worst fear.

Turn around and leave, idiot.

But his feet moved forward, treading as silently as possible over patchy grass too shaded to thrive. He moved close to the hammock and stared down, entranced.

Lisa Williams lay sleeping on her back, one hand pillowing her head, the other hanging limply off the hammock. She wore a lavender fleece tunic with a cream satin snowflake appliqué on the chest. Cream-colored leggings molded thighs and knees he knew looked terrific in a short dress. Half of her calves were encased in cream leather boots trimmed at the top with white fake fur. Her ankles were crossed, her feet so small they might've been a child's—except for the unmistakable woman's body above.

Dappled in sunlight, her glossy black hair tousled, she took his breath away. He seized advantage of the situation to look his fill.

Everything about her was exquisitely feminine. Her slim straight nose. Her delicate wrist and fine-boned hand. Her skin, so clear and pale she looked like Snow White awaiting the kiss of her prince to break the spell of a poisonous apple. He stared at her mouth, a plump cupid's bow parting slightly with each of her breaths.

And for the first time in Ross's life, he understood how a man could risk his career to woo and keep a woman happy.

He couldn't have said how long he stood there before her breathing changed, warning him to escape while he could. His feet stayed planted. Her lashes trembled, then swept up. Drowsy dark eyes met his and warmed in pleasure.

Then invitation.

His slamming heart threatened to crack his ribs. He lowered his gaze to her mouth and leaned down slowly. A small palm gently cupped his jaw…then almost shoved the back of his skull between his shoulder blades.

"What are you *doing?*" he heard through ringing ears and waves of pain.

She tumbled off the hammock and stood glaring up at him, her fists clenched. "You *pervert!* How *dare* you try to kiss me when I'm sleeping? What is your *problem?*"

"At the moment, whiplash." He grimly tilted his head this way and that in a test for serious damage.

"Well what do you *expect,* sneaking up on a woman and taking advantage of her when she's most vulnerable? You're lucky I didn't have my Mace handy.''

Suppressing a shudder, he set his hands at his waist, his own temper rising. ''I went to the front door and no one answered, so I thought maybe everyone was back here. Where are Kara and Esther?''

''At Taylor Fine Foundations. Kara takes her grandmother there every Saturday for an hour or so to visit with Carol. And don't change the subject. You really scared me just now.''

Like hell! ''Look, I apologize for startling you, but not for trying to kiss you. If ever a woman was begging to be kissed, it was you just now.''

She looked down at her frivolous boots and shook her head, looked up to the heavens and huffed in disgust, looked straight at Ross and made him wish he'd stayed in his cheerless apartment.

''Of all the arrogant, asinine, *offensive* statements I've heard a man make, that's got to top the list. Begging to be kissed? God, you sound like a bad novel. Does that line really work on all your other women?''

He bristled. ''What makes you think I have a lot of women?''

She flushed. ''A man like you normally does.''

''A man like me,'' he repeated, narrowing his eyes.

Something in her expression told him it wasn't

the insult he'd first thought. He barely noticed the sound of a car pulling into the driveway.

"You seem to have me all figured out. Wish I could say the same about you. Why are you trying so hard to antagonize me, Lisa?"

Her eyes grew huge in her face. "I don't know what you mean."

His irritation had magically vanished. "Oh, I think you do. I think you wanted to kiss me. Wanted to so much it nearly scared your little princess boots right off. So you had to make me mad to keep your distance."

A car door slammed. Then another.

"That's ridiculous," she said weakly.

"No, you were right to be scared, and I'm glad you pushed me away. Because if I'd kissed you—" he saw her lips part and almost growled in frustration "—you wouldn't have wanted me to stop, I promise. You wouldn't have appreciated an interruption."

"Mr. Hadley!" Esther exclaimed delightedly. "Kara said that was your car out front. I'm so glad we came home early."

Lisa's lashes fluttered down.

Ross turned toward the gate and the dear woman smiling a warm welcome.

"Me, too," he said, forcing a smile.

But for the life of him, he didn't know whether he was grateful or disappointed.

CHAPTER NINE

BY WEDNESDAY MORNING, Ross had convinced himself he was grateful. He couldn't afford distractions. There was too much riding on the next few weeks.

He drove through KLUV-TV's entrance gates and pulled into his reserved space under a dark-green awning. Entering the shade never failed to give him a thrill. He'd worked like hell to earn one of these thirty elite spaces.

That first July morning seven years ago, fresh from Buffalo and eager to ride the coattails of a promising new independent station in a top-ten market, he'd parked with other low-level employees in the uncovered spaces. At noon he'd walked out to his car and innocently reached for the door handle.

His palm had sizzled like steak on a grill.

Through a haze of pain at the emergency medical clinic, he'd vowed to park in the shade at this station one day. He would also develop and produce shows that earned him Emmys—or die trying. The effort hadn't finished him off yet, but it sure had killed his marriage.

Eventually he and Sally had realized he loved his job more than he did her. Two years ago, she'd returned to Buffalo and promptly married an electrician who kept regular hours.

Sliding out from behind the wheel now, Ross hoped Sally's new husband kept her warm through the Antarctic winters. Honest to God he did.

He grabbed his suit jacket, locked the Mercedes and headed for the sprawling one-story building housing his hopes and dreams. KLUV-TV was a growing power among television stations in the city. In recent years, original "ask the expert" shows on dating, marriage, homemaking and parenting had added unique spice to the programming.

Capturing an unserved market and positioning the station as "The Relationship Channel" had been his idea. A real boon to his career. Station owner Gerald "Da Man" Freedman loved Ross, and Ross intended to keep it that way.

He pushed through double glass doors into a small plush lobby. Green marble-tiled floor. Two seating areas defined by inset taupe carpet. Club chairs upholstered in a geometric taupe, green and rose pattern. A sleek contemporary security kiosk fashioned of green marble and brushed chrome.

As planned, visitors received the impression of a

prosperous station poised to dominate the market in the new millennium.

He approached the security kiosk briskly. No one, employee or visitor, got past the grizzle-haired guard without checking in and exchanging a few words first.

"Morning, Jim. You see the Rockets game last night?"

The retired police officer's face broke into a huge grin. "You mean that three-point buzzer beater? Man, was that sweet or what?"

Ross signed his name on the check-in sheet and smiled. "Damn straight. I won ten bucks from Tim Dawson. When he comes in, you tell him his precious Lakers choked, and I'm waiting to collect, okay?" The general sales manager, an L.A. transplant, made a real pain of himself during basketball season.

Jim's widening grin said he agreed.

"Oh, and I'm expecting Travis Malloy and Kara Taylor in an hour. No need to call me. Send them into the studio, if you would."

"You got it, Mr. Hadley. How's the new show comin' along?"

The station was a regular soap-opera community. Everybody knew everybody else's business, especially that of individuals whose success or failure affected multiple jobs.

"It's coming along great. Kara and Travis are

naturals. I've got a really good feeling about this one, Jim. I think it'll be a winner right out of the gate.''

''Me, too, Mr. Hadley. There's something about those two together...'' Jim's eyebrows formed one long fuzzy gray caterpillar, then separated. He shrugged. ''I can't really explain it, but if it comes across on camera, people will tune into the show.''

Speechless at this solid confirmation of his gut instincts from an unexpected source, Ross collected his composure and extended his hand for a brief shake. ''You just made my day—no, my *week*. Tell you what,'' Ross said expansively, ''I'll speak to 'Da Man' and see what I can do about getting you into our studio audience next Wednesday.''

''Really?'' Pleasure suffused Jim's face. ''Thanks, Mr. Hadley!''

Smiling, Ross nodded and walked toward the only door in the rosewood-paneled lobby. An instant before he grabbed the knob, he heard a distinctive click as Jim unlocked the entrance from his kiosk.

With a final wave, Ross walked into a world that had excited him from the time he'd interned at a small station near Syracuse College. Normally he took the long tunnel-like hallway to his left that bypassed the high-ceilinged warehouse-type studio. Today he opened a soundproof door and took the tour route through the "glamorous" part of the station. The area visitors wanted to see.

Even when no show was taping, like now, the ghostly props and completely furnished rooms were still magical. Visitors simply imagined the rows of arc lights blazing, the main floor cameras pointing at on-air personalities. Or maybe at themselves.

Ross paused beside a small stage set with six upholstered chairs lined in a row. The graphic designer had done a great job on the show's title. Mounted on foam board and suspended from a catwalk, the metallic gold letters in Old English type really popped out against the royal-blue curtain backdrop.

Backstage, a small dressing room, where Brad would ply his magic with make-up, and a slightly larger "greenroom," where guests would sweat off Brad's efforts, awaited occupants. Additional tiered seating would be borrowed from other areas next Wednesday to form the largest studio audience of any original KLUV-TV show.

Hear He, Hear She was the station's most ambitious program to date. Everyone loved the concept, but only Gerald's endorsement had persuaded the general manager and program director to let Ross tape a pilot using Travis and Kara as hosts. Ross knew at least four producers who hoped his baby would bomb, so they could step into the current Golden Boy's shoes.

A nerve jumped in Ross's cheek. He took a calming breath. He'd thought of every contingency, he assured himself. *Hear He, Hear She* would put him on the top rung. He could feel it in his bones.

The ones that shook more with each day he crossed off the calendar.

He'd thought of everything?

Ha! A million things could go wrong.

Pushing aside the thought, Ross continued on past Wardrobe and storage rooms, then a large glass window revealing the engineering room. Four monitors showing a deodorant commercial caught his attention. Manufacturers of personal hygiene products were big advertisers on The Relationship Channel.

The engineer on duty lifted a desultory hand in greeting as Ross walked by.

Ah, the glamour, he thought, reaching the end of the line for most guests. He opened the soundproof door to the buzz of conversation, ring of telephones and the start of his busy day.

TRAVIS PULLED into KLUV-TV's parking lot just as Kara was getting out of her Toyota. Even if he hadn't known what kind of car she drove, he would've recognized that hair from a mile away. It flashed silvery gold, the exact color of a leaping bass reflecting sunlight.

He'd told her so once, but she'd laughed, as if it

weren't a compliment. Which it was. About the highest he could give. The sight of a lunker breaking water was as beautiful as anything on God's earth.

She spotted his Jeep, pointed to the empty space beside her blue sedan and waited while he parked. They'd had three rehearsals at the station since the brainstorming session. Yet his nerves were strung tighter than a ten-pound test line hooked into Jaws.

Damn, but you'd think he'd be used to seeing her by now!

He got out of the Jeep and met her smile, struck speechless by her new haircut. Feathered bangs blended into tapered layers framing her high cheekbones and strong jawline. The rest fell thick and straight to her shoulders.

"Good morning," she said with a cheerful smile. "I like your haircut. Kent did a great job."

Travis's mood soured instantly. Grunting, he turned around and took his time locking the doors.

Better. He ought to be able to handle her new haircut now. His own was another story. Jake and Seth had taken one look and hooted their opinion.

His ears burning, Travis turned and headed for the station.

Kara caught up and fell into step beside him. "How was your drive in?"

"Long."

She recovered gamely. "At least it's a pretty day.

I'll bet the trees are gorgeous between here and the lake. The leaves are finally turning color.''

"The bass are finally hitting spinnerbait. So I *hear.*''

Her glance could've sliced tomatoes. "Look, I'm sorry about all these meetings and rehearsals. It's not like I have the time to spare, either. But we're committed to taping the pilot, and I really don't want to make a fool of myself next Wednesday. Do you?''

"Hell, Kara, I already have.''

They walked three steps.

"Okay, I'll bite,'' she blurted. "What do you mean?''

They'd reached the entrance. Travis held one door open and gestured grandly. "After you.''

She swept through with her chin held high. Tall. Graceful. Oozing "presence'' and the spicy floral perfume that crooked a come-hither finger under his nose. He followed helplessly to where she stood waiting for an explanation.

Wearing a burgundy turtleneck, wide black belt and slim black calf-length skirt, Kara couldn't be described as dainty.

But, oh brother, was she ever powerful.

The businessman seated to their left finally glanced at Travis, then hastily buried his face in a newspaper.

"Fine! Don't explain," Kara said, turning to head for the security kiosk.

Travis caught up with her in two strides. "What I mean is, Brad and his makeup brushes the other day were bad enough. Kent and his scissors from hell were the last straw. I can't *believe* I let Ross talk me into this haircut. I look like a damn fool."

She seemed startled, then amused. "Don't be silly. You look very handsome."

He couldn't suppress a burst of pleasure. Handsome was okay. He could live with that.

"Very stylish," she added.

Stylish? "That's it. I'm wearing a ball cap."

Laughing, she pulled up short in front of the kiosk and laid a forearm on the high ledge. "Jim, you remember what Travis looked like the first time we came into the station, don't you?"

The guard's bushy gray brows rose and fell. "Um, I guess so, Ms. Taylor."

"Take a good look at him now. Don't you like his new haircut better?"

Jim cocked his head and studied the cut in question a few seconds too long.

"My Evinrude cap," Travis said decisively. "The audience'll love it. It has a certain campy *je ne sais quoi.*"

"Campy is right. Puh-leez. That nasty thing?"

"Nasty? That cap has character."

"That cap has motor oil and fish guts all over it.

You'd clear the seats in five minutes.'' She glanced at Jim and pinched her nose meaningfully.

Travis pretended affront. ''Oh, so now it's too smelly for you? Funny how you lost your fine sensibilities out on my boat when your face was a French fry. All of a sudden, you couldn't wear my nasty cap fast enough.'' He looked at the guard man-to-man. ''I'd told her to bring a hat, but she didn't want to 'smush her hair.'''

Kara huffed. ''I wouldn't have *needed* a hat if you hadn't kicked the sunscreen into the lake.''

''Well, excuse me for not having eyes in my sneakers. It was an accident.'' Again, he sought the nearest male for support. ''I was standing on the bow fighting a ten-pound bass. She set this eight-ounce bottle of sunscreen right by my feet. I wear size thirteen shoes. You do the math.''

Grinning, Jim turned to Kara as if it were her serve, but she only stared thoughtfully at Travis's feet.

After calling them ''submarines'' she'd accused him of kicking the bottle in the water on purpose, of caring more about his precious bass than he did her. He'd taken her fishing with such high hopes. But everything about the sport he loved had either repulsed or bored the woman he'd loved more.

Kara looked up now and met his eyes, her expression cautious...and vulnerable. ''I was mortified that day. I did everything wrong. Backlashing my reel, not getting the net under your fish in time, wimping out on baiting my hook. Even the egg salad sandwiches I made were too salty to eat—'' she made a self-deprecating noise at his start of surprise ''—I saw you throw yours over the side when you thought I wasn't looking.''

She'd seen that?

''When you kicked the sunscreen overboard— granted, accidentally—I took out my frustration and hurt on you. I shouldn't have, though. It was unfair.''

Stunned, he didn't know what to say. Suddenly every cutting remark he'd made about her ineptitude, every show of impatience prompted by his own hurt came back to haunt him.

''Why didn't you tell me how you felt?'' he finally asked.

A sad smile entered her eyes. ''Since I couldn't make you proud of me, I decided your anger was better than pity.''

She hadn't wanted her grandparents' pity, either, for being selected to play Joseph because of her height. ''I can imagine you stirring up lots of different feelings in people, Kara. But pity isn't one of 'em.''

It sure wasn't what stirred to life as he watched unhappiness turn to gratitude and then, awareness of him as a man—not a painful memory.

''Excuse me,'' Jim blurted, obviously uncomfortable with the personal nature of their conversation. "I hate to interrupt, but Mr. Hadley is expecting you both in the studio right now."

Kara wrenched her gaze to smile brightly at the guard. "And here we stand reminiscing. Thank you for the reminder."

He smiled back, handing over a clipboard and pen. "Mr. Hadley says the show's comin' along great, by the way."

"I'm glad he thinks so. We're rehearsing what we can, but so much will depend on what the guests say and how we respond." She signed her name with a flourish and angled the clipboard toward Travis. "Wednesday will tell the true story. We'll try not to screw up in front of the *Houston Chronicle* television critic Ross invited to preview the show for readers. Right, Travis?"

He signed in, nearly tearing the paper before he eased up on the pen. "I'm trying not to think about it."

Jim and Kara laughed. She said a few more parting words along the same lines.

Like I was kidding, Travis thought, following her through two doors and into the studio.

They walked silently toward bright arc lights and activity at the far end. In previous rehearsals, they'd practiced using the microphones, looking directly into the camera lens and reading from a TelePromp-

Ter. They'd endured the attentions of a make-up artist, hair stylist and wardrobe consultant.

But Kara was right. Ultimately the show's success depended on their ability to think quickly on their feet.

The element of surprise made him damn jittery.

Up ahead through the tiered seats, he glimpsed a portion of stage, a slice of royal-blue curtain, a suspended gold *H* and part of an *E*. Ross was yelling at someone to cue the opening music. The score hadn't been ready at the last rehearsal.

The sudden blast of medieval trumpets stopped Kara and Travis in their tracks. As they blinked at each other, full orchestra music swelled in a stirring arrangement that would precede their entrance next Wednesday.

With horror, Travis saw his own doubts and misgivings creep into Kara's eyes.

"I've made a terrible mistake," she said in a small voice.

"Run that by me again?"

"I don't think I can do this."

If *she* sank, he was as good as drowned too. "Sure you can."

"No, I mean it, Travis. The whole thing hasn't seemed real until now. I've been fooling myself. My God, what have I done?" she said, groaning. "I can't get in front of a camera and studio audience and pull off any semblance of professionalism or poise.''

He moved closer and grasped her hands. ''Yes, you can.''

She shook her head miserably.

''You *can,* Kara. Because you're not doing any of this for yourself or for me. You're doing it for Esther—'' he rubbed her knuckles with his thumbs ''—and you won't let *her* down, now will you?''

Kara's panic-stricken expression slowly subsided. She took a deep breath, then another, her mouth firming. ''You're right, I won't.''

The resolve in her eyes faded into That Look. ''Thank you, Travis.''

Releasing her hands as if scalded, he didn't miss her instant stiffening. ''We'd better get in there,'' he mumbled.

But she was already walking toward the set.

He watched her book-on-the-head carriage a long moment, regretting that he'd hurt her, knowing he'd had no choice. That Look, the one that made him want to leap tall buildings in a single bound, would only lead to heartache and disappointment. For both of them.

Because sooner or later, no matter how much effort he put into the jump, he would fall short of her expectations.

CHAPTER TEN

"CLOSE YOUR EYES and don't breathe," Brad instructed, applying a final dusting of loose powder to Kara's face. "*Voilà!* Take a look at the next talk-show sensation, love. You're going to knock 'em dead out there."

Kara opened her eyes and studied her reflection in the brightly lit vanity mirror.

Three coats of mascara, expertly blended eyeshadow in shades from violet to plum, base foundation, liberal blush on her cheeks and glossy lipstick stared back. He'd told her that televison cameras and "hot" lighting tended to wash out faces that looked fine to the naked eye, but...

"You're sure I don't look like a clown?"

"Clown?" Brad puffed out his narrow chest. "Men will drool in their BarcaLoungers, women will rush out and get green contact lenses and plum eyeshadow in a hopeless effort to look like you, and this is the thanks I get?"

She laughed. "I'm sorry. I'm not used to wearing so much make-up, that's all. You did a wonderful job. Thank you."

The make-up artist inclined his spiky blond head, then stepped forward and whipped off the cape protecting her clothes.

After countless wardrobe changes for Ross, she'd modeled this Ellen Tracy suit in moss-green wool, worn with a high-necked shell in deep-plum. The jacket was long and fitted, the skirt slim and short. Too short for her comfort, but he'd taken one look at her legs and declared they'd found the perfect outfit.

She brushed a nonexistent piece of lint from her skirt. "How does Travis look?"

Brad huffed. "He went out on *that boat* of his yesterday. His face was wind-chapped again. I managed to tone down the ruddiness, but he nearly broke my wrist knocking the eyeliner brush away. Just look at this!" He unbuttoned and pushed up the cuff of his billowing shirt sleeve.

Thinking he sounded more thrilled than angry, Kara eyed the angry red spot on his bony wrist. "Brad, if you came anywhere near Travis with an eyeliner brush, you're lucky to escape with only a bruise."

"Ah, but what I could've done to those tiger eyes...." With a dreamy expression, Brad rolled down and rebuttoned his sleeve, then shook his head and clucked. "When he sees the tape of the show, he'll regret not trusting me."

"Well I, for one, am glad he didn't trust you. It

would be embarrassing for his eyes to be prettier than mine.''

Brad chuckled, but didn't disagree.

The dressing-room door opened and Lauren stuck her head inside. ''They're through prepping the audience, Brad. Travis is having a heart attack. Get Kara out here fast.''

Kara's stomach executed a series of flip-flops any gymnast would envy.

''I could do CPR,'' Brad said hopefully.

The associate producer snorted. ''Not unless you have a death wish.''

''It might be worth it.''

Lauren rolled her eyes at Kara, did a double take, then promptly rushed forward and helped her out of the chair. ''Easy, girl. Don't fall apart on us now.'' The harried woman guided Kara through the door as if she were an invalid. ''Pretend this is rehearsal and you'll be fine. Remember, we can edit out any major goof-ups when we add commercials later. Just keep the discussion lively, give us forty-five minutes of good tape and we'll be ecstatic.''

Gee, why was I worried?

''I'm okay, Lauren, really. Thanks. Go do what you have to do.'' Kara pulled away.

''You sure?''

''Go.''

Lauren nodded gratefully and rushed off. Kara

searched the darkened backstage and headed for two men standing in the left wing.

But her eyes remained glued on one.

Yowza! No wonder Brad had considered flirting with death.

The only time she'd seen Travis dressed up had been the afternoon of their wedding. They'd driven directly from the department store to the courthouse, ripping the price tags from his slacks and sports coat along the way. She'd thought then that no man could appeal to her specific aesthetic tastes more perfectly than her groom.

She'd been wrong.

Wearing a dark navy suit, the cut European and tapered, the material expensive, Travis looked tall, impossibly broad-shouldered and commanding. The "stylish" short haircut he'd bemoaned drew attention to his well-shaped head and strong square jaw, leaving enough rakish spill over his forehead to make her fingers itch to smooth it back. Despite Brad's efforts, Travis's squint lines and weathered tan marked him as an outdoorsman. The effect was devastating.

He turned as she approached, his gaze sweeping her up and down.

She thrilled to the gleam of appreciation in those tiger eyes. Through the hum in her blood she vaguely heard Ross giving last-minute instructions, details she'd heard ad nauseam. Yadda-yadda-yadda. Buzz-buzz-buzz.

"You look beautiful," Travis said, cutting through static loud and clear.

Her confidence soared. "Thank you. So do you. I'm glad you nixed the cap."

"I didn't. Nancy hid it." He grimaced ruefully. "That'll teach me to grumble my threats out loud."

Kara laughed, and his eyes flared.

Flushing, she looked away, feeling vibrant and attractive and, yes, *powerful*. No matter what else she thought about Travis, she'd never questioned his intelligence or courage. If she had to face the audience growing restive just out of sight, there was no one she'd rather have by her side than him.

She looked up, hiding nothing from her expression. "Ready?"

And suddenly he looked invincible. "As much as I'll ever be."

They turned as one to Ross, who'd stopped talking to watch them with obvious excitement.

"Excellent! Hold that mood," he ordered, cueing the floor manager to begin the show.

Trumpets blared, the theme music swelled. A technician scurried forward with two cordless microphones and handed one to each host. As they walked toward center stage, Kara mouthed, "Careful," then pretended to bash her mike on Travis's head.

They were both smiling broadly as they entered the audience's view, reached a spot about ten feet in front of the empty guest chairs and turned.

Blazing arc lights blinded Kara to individual faces, but Gram was out there somewhere, along with Major McKinney, Lisa, Nancy and Travis's entire family. She shoved the unnerving thought aside and focused on the center floor camera.

Inches below the lens, the TelePrompTer scrolled a script she knew by heart. "Good afternoon, ladies and gentlemen, and welcome to *Hear He, Hear She,* the show where men and women have equal voice and the opportunity to understand each other better. I'm Kara Taylor, one of your hosts. I'll be representing the woman's point of view during discussions with our guests."

"And I'm Travis Malloy, your other host. The one representing the voice of reason."

He paused to let that sink in and flashed a devilish grin at Kara, continuing only when the chuckles faded. "During the next hour, we'll hear from three couples who believe they have a communication problem in their relationship. But whether it's her fault or his...or simply the difference in how men and women interpret situations and conversations, remains to be seen. We'll let you be the judge."

Kara picked up her cue. "We want to emphasize that we're not trained counselors or linguists, nor do our opinions reflect those of this station or of anyone but ourselves. However—'' she glanced challengingly at Travis ''—I think you'll soon find out who the *true* voice of reason is around here.''

The chuckles this time were louder and lasted longer, as if the audience was warming to the spirit of friendly rivalry.

She swept the faceless mass with a bright smile. ''We'll also be asking for responses from you wise folks in our studio audience. So don't be shy when we head your way.''

Ignoring the ripple of nervous mumbling, she looked directly into the floor camera. ''Now, without further ado, please welcome our first couple, Helen and Jerry Whitaker.''

An applause cue card prompted the audience to clap at the arrival onstage of an attractive couple in their late forties, well dressed in business office attire. As they settled into chairs, the house lights came up.

Kara and Travis headed down a short ramp toward the tiered seats and split apart.

During rehearsal, negotiating the narrow aisle up into the empty seats had been difficult enough to give her nightmares. Totally justified, she thought now, acutely conscious of the camera following her progress.

She blocked out the audience and began to climb, a task that in high heels and a narrow skirt—without watching her feet and with any modicum of grace—required exceptional balance, supreme concentration and, most of all, an unobstructed aisle. Almost there. Two more steps and she could turn.

Her toe hit something hard. She stumbled and clutched the nearest support, a brawny shoulder attached to the muscular body of a man she'd last seen as a boy of nineteen.

Jake Malloy grinned apologetically and withdrew his sneaker another inch. Her quick glance down the row confirmed three more pairs of equally large feet. Straightening, she scanned the trademark crooked grins of Seth, Cameron and John, respectively, with Nancy a stunning bookend.

A rush of bittersweet affection held her mute. Thank goodness it was Travis's turn to speak!

Standing amid the far section of the audience, Travis continued the introduction.

"The Whitakers have been married for twenty-six years and have two sons in college. She's a legal secretary, he's a realtor specializing in commercial properties. Helen, Jerry, welcome to *Hear He, Hear She*."

The couple smiled nervously and mumbled thank yous.

Travis focused on the husband. "Jerry, I understand that you and your wife took a long weekend recently and rented a cabin in Lost Maples National Park. You both agree the trip was great until the last day, and then your stories begin to differ. Why don't you tell us your version of what happened?''

Jerry flicked a glance at his wife. ''She can't interrupt while I'm talking, right? I mean, she does that at home, but she can't here. That's the rule, isn't it?''

Recovering her wits, Kara broke in. ''Yes, it is. But as her spokesperson, I'm allowed to comment at will. And I must say, Jerry, I have a strong premonition we'll be able to offer you some helpful communication tips.''

While the audience laughed, Jerry flushed and smoothed his tie.

''Don't let them intimidate you,'' Travis advised. ''Tell us what happened that last day.''

Nodding, Jerry cleared his throat. ''Well, we'd had a great time, like you said. But on our last morning, she jumped on my case right after breakfast about how we have to start packing, and the barbecue pit needs cleaning, and the trash taken to the Dumpster, and the beds stripped and the kitchen mopped—as if they don't pay maids to do that when we leave—and all these other chores I *know* we have to do...only not right then.''

''Why not?''

''Because we still have hours left of a beautiful day to enjoy. So I say to her, why don't we pack a lunch and go for a last hike, take the short trail up to a small lake we haven't seen yet? Three hours, tops, round-trip.''

"So there would still be a half day left after the hike?''

"Right. But she says that's not enough time, that there's too much to do. She wants to get home by dark.'' Jerry blew out a frustrated breath. "Jeez, I went there to get *away* from all that hurry-up, rush-rush stuff. She was sucking me right back into stress mode.''

"Hey, I hear ya, buddy. So what did you do?''

Jerry shot his rigid wife a baffled look, then shrugged. "I went on a hike without her.''

Kara added her groan to the collective feminine swell of protest.

Travis held up a calming hand. "Whoa, now, ladies. Let's hear all the facts. Jerry, are you saying you went stomping off and left Helen with all the work?''

Jerry bristled. "No! I asked her to come with me two more times, but she just kept throwing clothes into suitcases and getting more upset. She was being totally unreasonable. Finally she yelled at me to go on without her...so I figured I'd give her some space and time to cool off.''

"Sounds like a good plan—except for leaving her with the chores.''

"I told her to leave the heavy chores for me and I'd do them when I got back.''

"Hmm. Seems fair to me. Anybody else have a comment? No, you ladies will get your turn later. Yes, sir, you in the blue shirt. Give us your name, please." Travis stretched his mike across three people, one of them Gram, to reach a familiar silver-haired man.

"Wayne McKinney," the Major answered. "I wanted to congratulate Jerry for living in the moment, instead of fretting about the future. When he gets to be my age, he'll remember his walk to a beautiful lake much more than he will arriving home by dark."

Spontaneous applause erupted. Gram smiled proudly at her companion.

Kara glanced at the stage and frowned. What about *Helen's* memory? From her wounded expression, it would be far less pleasant than Jerry's. Kara had certainly never forgotten all the times she'd felt abandoned and left to "fret" about her shortcomings, Gram's health and the fate of the family business.

"Good point," Travis praised the Major. "Anyone else have a comment? Yes, wait a sec and let me get there."

He moved up four steps to a young man being jabbed in the ribs by a buddy pointing to the nearest TV monitor. Both wore University of Houston ball caps. Catching sight of himself on screen, the first student reddened and shoved his snickering friend.

"Tell us your name and what's on your mind," Travis said, then tilted the mike.

"Um, Adam Trent. I was just wondering what happened when Jerry finished his walk. I mean, if I'd left my girlfriend alone like that, I'd've been doing everything *else* alone from then on. And I mean everything."

When the rumble of male chuckles faded, Travis turned toward the stage. "Jerry, was Helen still upset when you got back to the cabin?"

"Oh, yeah," Jerry said fervently. "She'd already packed the car and done all the chores by herself. Wanted me to feel as guilty as possible. Didn't say a word when I thanked her—just gave me the silent treatment. Not only then, but on the four-hour drive home."

"Ahh, the suffering martyr bit," Travis said in an all-too-knowing tone. "That can be rough to sit through."

Kara stiffened.

"Actually, it wasn't too bad."

"No?" Travis studied Jerry's sheepish smile, then broke into a slow grin. "What was the score?"

"Twenty-one to zip, Cowboys. First time in years I've listened to a whole game on the radio uninterrupted."

Oh, the men thought *that* was hilarious. Especially Travis. Helen's good-sport smile trembled at the edges, squeezing Kara's heart.

When he could be heard, Travis said, "This seems like a pretty cut-and-dried story to me. Jerry shouldn't be faulted for wanting to enjoy his last morning of vacation."

"No, he shouldn't," Kara agreed, turning all heads her way. "But how about for unnecessarily hurting his wife?"

Feminine murmurs of approval greeted her question.

Travis's jovial expression grew alert and wary. "If she was hurt, she shouldn't have been."

Kara bit back her first response and chose her words carefully. "He left Helen in a state of extreme distress to go off on a tra-la hike, and then didn't bring up the subject once during a four-hour drive. Don't you think that was a tad insensitive?"

"She was the one giving him the silent treatment, remember?"

"Ah, yes. 'The suffering martyr bit,' as you so eloquently put it. Did it ever occur to you that maybe—just maybe—Helen's 'suffering martyr bit' was a sign that she was, oh, let me make a wild guess...*suffering?*"

Applause broke out. A loud, "You go, girl!" prompted laughter and more ladylike applause.

Travis snatched up the gauntlet. "It occurred to me that a *man* in Helen's situation would've spent the hours Jerry went walking reviewing the facts. One. There was time to hike to the lake and still drive home by dark. Two. Jerry was willing to do his share of the chores. Conclusion—getting upset was 'unreasonable.' Remaining upset and silent would be melodramatic and doing the 'suffering martyr bit.'"

Holding Kara's gaze, he smiled without humor. "In other words, a *man* in the same situation would've *gotten over it already* instead of holding a grudge."

The boisterous male whistles and cheers really got on Kara's nerves. From the annoyed expressions of most women in the audience, she wasn't alone.

"You're missing the point," Kara said ineffectually.

Nancy hissed at the Malloys to quiet down. Other women did the same to their men.

The noise calmed, and Kara addressed Travis again. "I understand—I think all the women here today understand—the thought process and logic behind Jerry's behavior. But the point I'm making is not that Helen was rational and Jerry didn't have a legitimate gripe, but that she *wasn't* rational. And there was a *reason* she wasn't that Jerry didn't bother to find out.

"She needed to talk about her feelings. He chose to dismiss them as unreasonable and go about his business, hoping the whole episode would blow over. If a man does that consistently to a woman, she begins to think he doesn't care enough to exert any effort in maintaining their relationship…''

Kara trailed off, realizing how passionate she sounded, how silent the audience was, how intently Travis watched her above an expanse of curious gazes.

Flustered, she turned to the stage. "Helen, if I've misinterpreted your reaction, I apologize, and now is the time to correct me. I think we'd all like to hear your version of what happened."

The audience's attention shifted to Helen. No one checked the monitors, whispered to neighbors or watched the technical crew. At some point the men and women in the audience had become completely engrossed in the unfolding story.

As a camera zoomed in for a close-up, Helen's gaze skittered to Kara and clung.

Kara smiled encouragingly. "You ate breakfast, and then felt compelled to begin packing. Can you tell us why?"

"When I woke up, all I could think about was the stack of depositions waiting on my kitchen table for me to type that night. At least three hours' worth of work." Her voice gained conviction and strength. "I *should* learn to live in the moment. I know that. But I didn't want to be up late since I'd have to leave for the office the next morning by six." Helen grimaced in distaste.

"That early?"

"I work downtown. Traffic is stop and go," she explained. "Anyway, after breakfast, my stomach was twisting and my muscles were knotted and there were a million things to do before we could get on the road. And Jerry decided he wanted to go on a hike. Right then—not after we finished the chores, like I suggested."

Kara raised her brows. "He forgot to mention that little detail."

"Yes, he did." Helen glanced wryly at her squirming husband, then offered a rueful smile. "In his defense, I was ragging him pretty badly. I wasn't being…reasonable. He was right about that. Have you ever listened to yourself say things like it was somebody else talking, and you had no control over your mouth?"

Kara thought of her first year of marriage. "Yes, I've done that."

"Well, that's how it was with me that morning, ranting about chores. Shoot, even *I* wanted to get away from me," Helen admitted, her endearing candor earning laughter and goodwill from both genders.

"I know it doesn't make sense, but all the time I was pushing and pushing, I didn't want him to actually leave. I don't walk away from *him* when he snaps *my* head off—which is plenty, believe me."

Kara detected exasperation, but no malice, in

Helen's tone. "Okay, turnabout's fair play. What *do* you do?"

"You mean after I snap his head off right back?" This time Jerry laughed along with the crowd.

Helen smoothed her skirt with a thoughtful expression. "I suppose I try and figure out what's bothering him that's putting him in a bad mood."

Bingo. "So if Jerry had probed to see if something else was troubling you, instead of deciding you were being unreasonable and giving you space, you wouldn't have been hurt?"

"Objection," Travis interrupted in a droll tone. "Counsel is leading the witness."

Kara had to laugh.

"Sustained," she acknowledged. But she didn't abandon her line of questioning. "Helen, why would the mere thought of returning to work twist your stomach and knot your muscles and make you miserable enough to act like a shrew?"

Helen blinked, then carefully avoided her husband's startled stare.

"She loves her job," Jerry answered for his wife.

Helen met his gaze and teared up instantly.

His shock and concern appeared genuine. "Don't you?"

Swiping a thumb beneath one eye, she shook her head. "I know the money's good, and I'd never find a better benefits package anywhere else, but I *hate* the drive in. And Mr.—" She broke off, obviously realizing television wasn't the forum to name specific people. "I guess it all got to me that last morning."

He looked shaken. "Why didn't you tell me that instead of complaining about chores?"

"My God, Jerry, I've lived with you twenty-six years. Kara only met me today, yet *she* found out. How do you think that makes me feel about our marriage?"

The words teetered on the edge of disaster. Kara hadn't intended to break up the couple's marriage, for heaven's sake! Her mind scrambled for a way to atone for her brash interference.

"Back up a minute, Helen," a deep voice commanded.

One of the cameras and all heads swung toward Travis.

"You're assuming Jerry didn't care enough about your feelings to probe beneath your surface complaints. I think it simply never occurred to him those complaints *could* be a smoke screen.

"See, most men don't want to be asked questions when they're upset. They want time and space alone to sort through thoughts. Then, if they feel the need to talk, they usually come right out and state the problem without circling all around it."

Both Helen and Jerry waited expectantly.

"And your succinct point would be…?" Kara couldn't resist asking.

Travis spared her a dark glance. "Women need to yell 'Fire!' right away, not when our butt's already toast."

The audience roared.

So much for dignity, Kara thought, shaking her head at his sexy unrepentant grin. Her mouth twitched, then curved up, then grinned back. What was a red-blooded girl to do?

Gary, the floor manager, gave Kara an urgent signal.

Rats! They'd run too long without breaking for a commercial.

She forced a bright smile for the camera. "Thank you, Travis, for that hot communication tip. When we come back after a word from our local sponsors, we'll hear from two more couples on the new show everyone's talking about...*Hear He, Hear She.*"

The red light winked off. An excited buzz commenced as the audience talked to seat neighbors about what they'd seen and heard.

Kara sagged and inwardly groaned. She'd stumbled climbing the stairs. She'd looked into the wrong camera more than once. Oh, man, she hadn't allowed any *women* in the audience to speak! How could she have forgotten?

A hand squeezed her arm. She looked down into Jake's admiring dark eyes. Of the three younger brothers, he looked most like Travis.

"Hang in there, Kara, you're doing great. So is

Travis. You two look as if you've been doing this for years.''

"Liar.'' She smiled and patted his hand. "But thanks, anyway.''

Seth leaned forward, caught her eye and winked. "I thought it'd be boring—ooph! *Hey!*'' Rubbing his ribs, he shot a murderous look at Cameron. "You didn't let me finish. I was gonna tell her it isn't boring at all. I'm actually learning new stuff.''

As Seth turned innocent blue eyes back to Kara, his elbow rammed into solid muscle beside him.

During the ensuing contained scuffle, Kara pondered the fact that she'd learned new stuff, too.

Sudden applause and a swell of theme music warned her that taping would restart at any second. She would have to examine and process her feelings later, after the show finished.

If she had the courage.

CHAPTER ELEVEN

AFTER THE SHOW, Nancy had the choice of waiting for Travis to finish taping station promo spots, or accepting John's gracious offer to taxi her to Bass Busters. No contest. For the first time in months, she would have him all to herself.

Yet once she climbed inside the Blazer, darned if she knew what to do with him.

So she talked.

She praised Kara and Travis lavishly, repeated compliments she'd overheard from people in the audience, speculated on the show's future, wondered aloud if Meg and Brian, the last couple on *Hear He, Hear She,* would get married or drift apart.

During a pause, she intercepted John's curious glance and turned to stare out the passenger window.

She'd learned from today's show that most women discussed recent experiences as a way to process information, to explore feelings, to arrive at a conclusion as they talked. Nancy supposed she did that, too. With Travis.

With his father, she worried too much about sounding foolish or dull to "think out loud." Normally she stuck to three subjects she knew interested him. Bass Busters, Malloy Sporting Goods and Jeremy.

Heaven forbid she should bore the almighty John Malloy.

Nancy tensed.

When she realized she was literally holding her breath, something inside her snapped.

Idiot! What had she expected? To be smote by lightning? He was only a man, for pity's sake.

An exceptional one, true, having raised four sons to adulthood with firm but loving guidance, never shirking his duty, building a reputable business along the way. He was the antithesis of the lover who'd abandoned her and their unborn child.

Still, he *was* mortal flesh and blood.

And yet for three years she'd watched and waited and done "the suffering martyr bit" while he'd remained kind, friendly and impersonal. In a convoluted way, she'd enshrined him as surely as he had the memory of his beloved wife, Kathryn.

Ironic. And pitifully sad.

Especially since her blinders had prevented her from doing the right thing by Travis.

"You're sure quiet over there all of a sudden," John observed, his deep voice amused.

She watched the thickening pine trees flash by

outside the window. "I figured you could use a break. Sorry for chattering."

"Actually, I was enjoying the conversation."

She twisted around to gauge his seriousness.

Eyes straight ahead, one hand draped casually over the top of the wheel, his stomach flat and his legs long, John was the mold from which four beautiful male specimens were cast. At fifty-four, despite his silvering hair, he looked as fit and virile as his sons.

He glanced over and caught her staring.

Awareness pulsed in his dark eyes. He looked back at the road, and she wondered if she'd imagined it.

One corner of his mouth lifted. "I've never heard you chatter before. I like listening to you."

If she didn't know better, she'd almost think he was flirting!

She forced the breathlessness from her voice. "In that case, there's something else I want to discuss. It's about Travis and Kara."

In the space of a blink, John's expression shuttered. "What about them?"

So much for her fantasy. "Did you notice the way he looked at Kara during the show? He couldn't manufacture that kind of intensity on demand."

"She's a beautiful woman."

"Yes. But I've never seen him look so alive, so

focused completely on another person. I suspected it when she first came to the fishing camp. Now that I've seen them together again, I'm sure he feels more than attraction.''

A skeptical noise low in his throat answered her statement.

''Travis is still in love with her,'' Nancy insisted. ''The question is, how do we help him accept and deal with that?''

His striking dark eyebrows lifted comically high, then lowered into a thunderous ledge. ''We *don't*. What's past is past.''

It was her turn to growl.

''Look, Nancy, you didn't see Travis hit rock bottom when Kara left Lake Kimberly to move back in with her grandmother. I talked myself blue in the face trying to get him to bend a little, to see gray instead of black and white, but he wouldn't listen to reason. He was hurting too much. And so depressed I drove to the camp and checked on him daily.''

Nancy's heart ached for them both.

And a little for herself.

''He scared ten years off my life those first six months. Do you understand what I'm saying?''

She met his probing glance with a small smile. ''My first trimester, Dad used to 'forget' things he needed from upstairs twice a day. Then he'd poke his head inside my room to say hello. So yes, I understand what you're saying."

Compassion softened his features.

"But like me, Travis healed."

John's frown returned. "Exactly. And it took him years to laugh and joke again. *Years.* Damned if I'm going to interfere now with the peace he's found. Kara deserves better than that, too."

"But what if she still loves him?"

"That's irrelevant."

Nancy gaped. "How can you say that?"

"Because it's true. She loved him before and still divorced him. The fishing camp is Travis's life, and she wants no part of it."

"Maybe it wasn't the life she wanted eight years ago. But people do change, you know. They get hurt, they heal, they move on to a better understanding. *Some* people even risk getting hurt all over again."

"And some people are smarter than that."

"Oh, please." Nancy reached to flip back her hair and remembered she'd taken special pains to achieve a perfect French twist. As if he would notice. "That's not smart. That's chicken. When are you going to realize that Travis isn't *you?*"

The hand draped casually over the steering wheel shifted into a death grip only a crowbar could pry loose. "Well, that's cryptic. Care to explain what you mean?"

"I don't know. Can you take the heat?"

"Try me."

Three years of banked and smoldering emotion burst into flames. "I mean that *his* wife isn't dead and sanctified to the point no other woman can ever measure up. I mean that *he* might be persuaded to take a chance and love a second time. I mean that *you've* encouraged him to stay insulated and safe, when any *smart* person would realize that's not living. That's only existing. Do you honestly want to deny him what you and Kathryn shared?"

His jaw bulged once. "You have no frame of reference for what Kathryn and I shared."

The insult skewered deep. She flounced around to face the front, her vision blurred. "You're right. But I wish I did."

"Nancy—"

"No, let me finish. I *want* to know what it's like to share a love that transcends life. It may never happen, but I won't close myself off to the possibility, or let Travis stay in an emotional cocoon, either. We both deserve what you and Kathryn shared—" she shot him a meaningful glance "—whether you think so or not!"

Staring blindly ahead, her breathing harsh in the charged silence, she sensed every glowering look thrown her way, heard every scathing word he held back. Lord, why hadn't she kept her mouth shut?

She drew a shaky breath filled with the breezy

aftershave she loved, plus a musty smell she didn't. Dirty socks—or worse—lurked somewhere in the back, possibly growing mildew. Jake used the Blazer like a sports locker.

Her vision gradually cleared. She was startled to see they were on the winding blacktop road past the Fisherman's Cafe. Talk about tunnel vision. She hadn't even known they'd exited the freeway!

Minutes later, the Blazer slowed and approached the gate to Bass Busters Fishing Camp. She reached for her seat belt.

"Wait," John ordered, shifting the truck into park.

She turned in question.

His tobacco-brown gaze smoked a trail from the top of her upswept hair to her high heels. "You'll ruin your hose. I'll get the damn gate."

He unbuckled his seat belt and flung it aside, jerked open the door and stomped off, plowing straight through a thatch of high weeds and cockle-burs.

O-o-oh, he was mad.

Nancy shivered, not unpleasantly.

His gaze had been anything but friendly, impersonal or insulated.

For all his anger, she'd seen something else in his eyes that stunned and thrilled her, made her glad she'd worn her clingy blue silk dress that reached

above the knees. Which he'd not only noticed...
he'd also liked!

She hugged the information close as he manhandled the gate open, trudged back to the idling Blazer, drove through and repeated the process in reverse. Throughout the winding drive to the camp, she considered what to do with her new knowledge.

Apologize and return to the status quo?

Intolerable!

Say nothing?

No. Too passive.

Deliver more of her opinion on idolizing a memory when a warm breathing woman loved him to distraction?

Hmm. Nancy risked a quick peek at John's implacable profile.

Scratch that. She'd won a skirmish and toasted his butt, but in a war he would incinerate her on the spot.

The truck broke into the cleared acreage of the camp. Lake Kimberly glittered east to west across the horizon, a glorious panoramic postcard so familiar she merely flipped down her visor, annoyed by the glare. Tires crunched against the crushed-shell driveway leading to the main house.

What to do, what to do?

In the end, John decided for her.

"I think it's best we forget this conversation and put it behind us, Nancy. I know you said some things you'll probably regret later.'' He braked to a stop, parked, and laid his hand behind her headrest. Where anger had radiated moments earlier, sincerity now oozed from his pores. ''Don't worry. I value your friendship too much to hold a grudge.''

Grudge? ''That's real big of you, John, but I don't regret a single thing I said. If that jeopardizes our friendship, then I guess our relationship will just have to change, won't it?'' Fumbling with her seat belt, she heard his buckle unlatch. ''No, don't bother, I'll get my own damn door.''

If she could only unbuckle her damn seat belt. Ah, at last! She looked up—and froze.

One hand still behind her headrest, his body curved, his face closer than she'd expected, he looked flustered and confused and thoroughly, irresistibly mortal.

What the hey?

Without giving herself time to think, she leaned forward and brushed her trembling lips once, twice, against his hard mouth. Sensation rocketed to her toes. She pulled back, quite unable to meet his eyes.

''Thank you for the ride,'' she managed in a strange voice before snatching up her purse and almost tumbling out of the truck.

She wobbled as fast as high heels over crushed shells would permit toward the front door, conscious of his stare the entire way. It took her forever to find her key chain among a jumble of cosmetics, another eternity to insert metal properly into the lock. She shoved her shoulder against wood, waved her hand vaguely in John's direction and shut herself inside, whirling to brace her dissolving spine against the door's welcome support.

Safe.

Oh-wow-oh-wow-oh-wow-oh-wow.

She'd kissed him!

Oh-wow-oh-wow-oh-wow.

Gradually her heartbeat slowed. She forced herself to review the drive here.

There'd been that moment of almost-maybe flirting. Then that searing head-to-toe inspection. She hadn't imagined *that.* And on the second brush of her lips, he'd gone unnaturally still, as if coiled and waiting to release tumultuous anger. Or possibly…passion?

The thought resonated with truth.

That's why she'd responded to the chaste kiss so strongly. She'd sensed the passion he fought to contain.

Well, well, well, Nancy thought, a wondering smile curving up her mouth. Their relationship had changed, all right. Lust wasn't "love that transcended life" by any means. But it was more than she'd had this morning. It was better than she'd ever expected to have. It might be superficial. It might be transient.

But, by God, it was a start.

KARA STUDIED HERSELF critically in the full-length bedroom mirror. The suit she'd worn yesterday for the pilot had been short, but this getup was…well, forget it.

That's what she got for raiding a petite woman's closet.

"I'm supposed to be a model, not a hooker," she complained, turning toward her fashion consultant.

Sprawled on her stomach and wearing overalls, one leg bent wishbone style, Lisa looked more like a child on her parents' bed than the owner of this upscale town house.

She raised her chin from a scrunched pillow and sniffed. "That's a Calendri original, I'll have you know. Only the classiest society women, film actresses and call girls wear his designs—if they have the body for it—and everyone admires their chic sophistication."

"Maybe you look chic in this. But *I* look like a slut. The neckline's too low, the hem's too short, and everything's way too tight."

"Not for a lingerie model. Good grief, those women prance around almost naked in prime-time television commercials and no one blinks an eye."

"Everyone's staring too hard at the prancing sluts to blink."

Lisa heaved a put-upon sigh. "You're really getting on my nerves. Over a half-million Houstonians will stare at your body when those catalogs start hitting mailboxes tomorrow. You'll take their money eagerly enough. Loosen up, for heaven's sake—no, for Vinnie's sake.''

"Oh, Vinnie will think I'm loose, all right, if I wear this outfit in public." Kara ignored her friend's glare and plucked fretfully at her chest and derriere.

"Vinnie has flown all the way from New York to take you to dinner and a club wearing *exactly* that kind of outfit. He wants you to look sexy, and he wants other men to see you looking sexy draped over his arm in public. That's a big part of his fantasy. Be glad he agreed to Thursday night. At least the crowds won't be huge."

"But I don't *feel* sexy. I feel like a—"

"Argh! Don't say it. You're playing a role, here, remember? You've got to look the part. Thank goodness you brought dressy flats that work. Smart thinking. He'll be a little taller than you. He'll love that."

"But what if I run into someone tonight who recognizes me? I'll be mortified."

Lisa raised a level gaze. "Kara. Hon. No offense, but who would recognize you? The show hasn't aired yet, so that's not an issue. And you're not a regular on the restaurant and nightclub circuit. You haven't even gone out since what's-his-name last year. What *was* his name?" Her brow furrowed.

"The guy who sold brassieres as cheap as *he* was. He took you to Denny's."

"Leave the poor man alone." Please.

"Hey, that was your description, not mi—oh! I remember now. *Harvey*. The perfect name." Lisa smothered a yelp of laughter with her pillow, then looked up, her dark eyes merry. "You said he had rabbit teeth and was so dull he was practically invisible." She dissolved into fresh laughter.

Telling her best friend everything had occasional drawbacks.

Kara folded her arms beneath her breasts and fought a smile. "We can't all be pursued by prospective junior partners in a big law firm."

"I'm sorry." Lisa took a deep, almost gigglefree breath. "I'm sorry. Really. I wouldn't laugh if you couldn't date dozens of men any time you wanted."

"Yeah. I'm just beatin' 'em off with a stick."

Sobering, Lisa pushed herself into a cross-legged sitting position. "This is me, remember? Don't play dumb. Those I'm-not-interested signals you give off to every attractive man within a thirty-yard radius are just as effective as a stick. Harvey happened to be boring enough for you to feel safe dating him. But face it, girlfriend. The Harveys of the world will never thrill you like Travis did. Like he still does."

Kara stiffened. "Travis doesn't thrill me."

Lisa remained silent, her gaze compassionate.

Spinning around to her reflection, Kara began tugging down the hem of her poly-spandex cream-colored skirt. "Okay, he does thrill me. But he's also as obsessed as ever with that Kimberly bitch, and I'm not about to try and break up their relationship again. I'll lose."

"Did you try and break them up a first time?"

Kara stilled. "What?"

"You said 'again.' As if when you were married, you wanted Travis to give up the lake and fishing camp. Did you give him an ultimatum? Is that why he never came after you?"

Kara scowled. "*No-o.* I can't believe you'd say that! You know I worked like a dog trying to make the place nice for guests. I even developed a five-year marketing plan to expand and modernize the camp." She met perceptive brown eyes in the mirror and experienced a twinge of unease. Irritation followed. "I'd suggest you stop analyzing my past and current thrills and take a look at your own. Ross spends as much time at KLUV-TV as Travis does on the lake."

"So? What does that have to do with me?"

Kara merely arched a brow.

Lisa's gaze faltered and dropped to the pillow in her lap. She punched it once. "Okay, Ross thrills me. I'll never let *him* know it. The man's ego is almost as big as Chad's."

"Ross is extremely confident, yes. Pompous, no. And too cute to stay mad at even when I am." Refocusing on her reflection, Kara lost her fond smile and fussed with the plunging sweetheart neckline of her ivory top. The puckered stretch velvet lost most of its pucker at the fullest part of her breasts.

Lisa's silence finally penetrated, and Kara thought back to her last comment. "Don't get me wrong. He doesn't thrill me. But I do like and admire him. He's as likely to implement suggestions from the station's security guard as from the program director. His first loyalty is to the show. But face it, girlfriend," she repeated Lisa's words and no-nonsense tone. "That's part of his allure for you."

"Excuse me?"

"He's a challenge. You've never known a man that didn't grovel at your dainty feet."

"Give me a break."

"Struck a nerve, did I?"

"Yes, but not the one you think."

The satin comforter rustled. Lisa appeared beside Kara in the mirror, looking mad enough to take on Goliath.

"*Enough* with the 'dainty' crap, already! I'm short, you're tall. They both have advantages and disadvantages. You're savvy enough to use your advantage for the business purpose of selling catalog lingerie. So *some* part of your brain recognizes you're not the same tall skinny teenager that boys never asked out. Or the wife who thought her husband would rather fish than be with her.''

Kara's arms fell limply to her sides, rendered useless by the spear through her heart.

''Oh, Kara.'' Exasperation and love resounded in Lisa's voice. ''Would you *look* at yourself, please? Not at the clothes. But at *you*.

''You're a photographer's dream. Most lingerie models would require soft-box lighting and body makeup. With you, I can shoot in broad daylight and your skin still looks poured from a milk carton. I don't have to manipulate camera angles to make your legs look longer. I don't have to experiment with key and fill light to exaggerate cleavage shadow. I can concentrate on creating the right mood for the merchandise shown.''

Hearing her attributes described in non-sexual terms helped Kara admit aloud what only her subconscious mind had acknowledged. ''All right. I have a decent body. Is that what you wanted to hear?''

''Hallelujah! Progress at last.''

''So *now* can I take this off and wear the dress I brought from home?''

The triumphant gleam in Lisa's eyes dimmed. ''And look like you're going to church? Depends on whether or not Vinnie has invoiced you yet for printing the *Mystery Woman* catalogs."

Rats.

"I didn't think so. Then you'd better stick with what you have on. It's perfect. We'll add some classy accessories if you're so worried about looking cheap." She bustled over to her sleek cherry-wood dresser and pulled forward a large jewelry box.

Watching her determined friend extract an exquisite baroque pearl pendant with delicate chain, matching earrings and square-cut emerald ring, Kara accepted defeat. Rejecting such generosity would hurt Lisa worse than looking like a slut would humiliate Kara.

"Come here and I'll help put these on you," Lisa ordered.

Minutes later, Kara tensed beneath a head-to-toe inspection.

Lisa's dark eyes shone with approval, then grew suspiciously bright. "You'll knock the breath out of him, hon. You look gorgeous and chic and very sexy."

Maybe tonight wouldn't be so bad.

"Except for your face."

Kara's budding excitement wilted. Thorns of doubt pricked her confidence. She'd worn too much makeup. She hadn't worn enough—

Small hands grabbed her shoulders and posi-

tioned her toward the dresser mirror. Her gaze ze-
roed in on the large pearl nestled between an inch
of visible cleavage.

"I said your face, Kara. Look at your expression.
It's embarrassed. If I had to reveal your face in the
Mystery Woman photos, the catalog would be a to-
tal failure. When I click the camera, your body says
'Come and get it' but your expression says 'Get me
out of here!'"

"I can't help it if I'm modest. And Vinnie's not
going to 'get' anything tonight but a big check from
Tony's." He'd made reservations for eight o'clock
at the preferred restaurant of prominent Houstonians.

"Of course he isn't. But he's got to think there's
a remote chance to get lucky. Think about Travis a
minute. He finds excuses to touch you, doesn't he?
You catch him staring as if he'd like to do more.
You're always wondering if he'll make a move to
kiss you, and that thrills you. He makes you feel
sexy."

The memory of tiger eyes burning possessively
accelerated Kara's heartbeat.

"*Yesss!* Hold that expression all night and you'll
need more than a stick to beat the men off. Did you
bring your Mace?"

Kara dragged her focus away from her lax
mouth, heavy lids and rosy flush. "What? Oh,
yes."

"Good." Lisa checked her watch. "You don't have to leave for another ten minutes. Now here's what I want you to do. Pretend Vinnie is Travis, and you're not the modest ladylike Kara Taylor, but the exotic seductive *Mystery Woman*. There's no Gram watching from a corner of your mind. You can be a vamp. You can be a flirt. You can be a sexy woman who likes men and shows it. You can be *powerful*. You can have fun. A lot of fun.

A strange excitement seized Kara. Did she dare?

"And last, but not least…" Pausing dramatically, Lisa grabbed a set of keys from the dresser top. "You can drive my car. Leave the top down. It's a little nippy, but you'll be fine with my cashmere shawl."

Kara stared mesmerized at the intoxicating freedom dangling in front of her nose.

"The front door key has a little red dot on it, see? Just let yourself in. I'll probably get up, but if not, we'll talk in the morning."

Gram knew Kara was spending the night. She could stay out till the clubs closed if she wanted. What harm could there be in playing the role to the hilt? No one but Lisa would ever know.

She slowly reached for the keys.

CHAPTER TWELVE

TRAVIS SLUNG AN ARM over the back of his chair, stretched his legs out a comfortable distance and thumbed a trickle of sweat from his long-neck Corona. His belly was full of Grub House mesquite-smoked brisket. Cameron and Jake bickered while Seth thought whatever he thought across the checkered tablecloth. And the pilot had gone well the day before.

For the moment, Travis was content.

This morning's *Houston Chronicle* had printed a glowing preview of the show that would air tomorrow, advising Houstonians to tune in. Ross was ecstatic. Even Travis's brothers seemed impressed. At least, Seth and Cameron did, and their opinion mattered most.

The two had spent today visiting Houston veterinary clinics and attending pre-scheduled business meetings, respectively. Seth, to gather ideas for the animal hospital he planned to build in Wagner, Texas, soon. Cameron, to capitalize on Malloy Marketing's growing buzz as ''a cutting-edge Austin agency prepared to tackle the new millennium's unique business challenges.''

When Travis had stumbled across that sentence in a *Time* magazine article on Texas-based companies, he'd damn near split his face grinning. Cam's polished charm, restless energy and business acumen were taking him far. Seth's quiet dedication and methodical one-step-at-a-time approach to goals were equally effective. The two seemed total opposites. Yet both were high achievers and a source of great pride to their father, who'd encouraged all of his sons to earn a college degree.

Travis had pursued a practical rather than higher education. His classrooms had been creek channels, reed shallows and open lake. His professors the topographical maps, hours upon hours of casting, and bass movements dictated by weather, spawning and feeding patterns. He'd never regretted his decision to forgo college. But he knew that Kara secretly had. That a white-collar professional was much closer to her ''ideal'' husband than the man she'd actually married.

As for Jake regretting anything…

Travis glanced at the brother currently balancing an up-ended Corona bottle on his nose. His jeans and football jersey looked slept in.

Jake, Jake, Jake. Lover of practical jokes, a good time and women. Combining all three in one experience was his idea of success. Oh, he helped Dad operate the store efficiently enough, but his heart wasn't in it. They were all still waiting to see what—or who—would eventually capture his sincere interest.

With a mental shrug, Travis took a swig of beer. Seth and Cam had phoned earlier and invited the other Malloys to join them for dinner. Jake was always game for driving into Houston. Their father almost never was. Since Travis hadn't known when he'd get another chance to talk to his brothers alone and all at once, he'd accepted.

Just then a full-figured forty-something waitress bustled by with a tray of food. Jake's head veered one way, his balanced beer bottle the other.

Cameron snatched the long-neck midair and inches from the cement floor. "Damn it, Jake, you're worse than a kid! Why don't you run away and join the circus so we can stop baby-sitting?" Setting the bottle far out of reach, he glanced at Travis. "Jeez. How do you *take* him?"

"Only in small doses. Any more than that is bad for his health."

"I try not to let him get to me. I really do," Cam told his Bud Light. "But then he acts like a two-year-old or a trained seal, and I lose it."

"That's what he wants."

All eyes turned to Seth, whose calm blue gaze matched treasured photographs of their mother.

Wearing a Western-cut shirt, Wranglers and boots, he looked right at home in the bunkhouse ambiance.

"When you don't react," he explained with a nothing-to-it shrug, "he gets bored and loses interest."

Cameron turned to raise a dark-blond eyebrow at the youngest Malloy. "That true, butthead?"

Pressing his elbows, forearms and palms together, Jake slapped his "flippers" together and barked like a seal.

Three hands reached for nearby missiles. A coaster, a French fry and a spoon launched simultaneously. The latter glanced off Jake's cheek and clattered against the floor.

"He-ey!" he protested, glaring at Cameron. "You could've put out my eye."

"Small price to pay for shutting you up."

"*Stop,*" Travis ordered, before they could get into it deeper. "I have something I want to discuss. I'm worried about Dad."

That got their full attention.

"Any of you notice anything…I dunno, different, about him lately?"

"Different how?" Jake asked, his dark eyes keen and intelligent, as if a mask had lifted.

"I don't want to influence you by getting specific. Maybe I'm just imagining things."

"He's real stressed about business dropping off," Cameron admitted. "And about budgeting so much money for the Thanksgiving weekend sale. 'Course, since you didn't totally suck eggs yesterday as a co-host, he probably feels better now about using you as a spokesperson for Malloy Sporting Goods commercials.''

Damn. "Did you set a date for the shoot yet?''

Tilting forward, the only son to inherit Kathryn's dark-gold hair pulled an appointment book from his rear pocket. He resettled and flipped through the pages.

Trust Cameron to make jeans and a black Polo shirt look as formal as a suit.

"Here it is. The first Saturday in November. Be at the store an hour before it opens to rehearse your lines while the crew sets up. We'll edit on Monday back in Austin, and express-ship the tapes to Houston stations on Tuesday.'' He flipped the book shut and shared a commiserating look with Travis. "Fun, fun, fun.''

And another fishing guide trip canceled.

Jake toyed with the greasy paper lining his empty food basket. "Dad nearly ripped my head off for trying to talk him into coming with me tonight. I think maybe something besides the store is bugging him.''

"He has the hots for Nancy,'' Seth stated with quiet conviction.

Travis, Jake and Cameron gaped.

"He has for years. He just won't admit it to himself."

"You're crazy," Travis muttered.

"Raving nuts," Cameron seconded.

"I don't know..." Looking thoughtful, Jake leaned back and propped a running shoe on his opposite knee. "When he got back to the store yesterday after driving Nancy home, he seemed pretty rattled. He went in the stockroom to check on a special-order fly rod and never came out. I found him staring at a case of plastic worms like it was a TV."

Seth's lips curved in a small smile, but he merely picked up his Coke.

"Come to think of it," Cameron said grudgingly, "I did see his eyes bug a little at that silk dress she wore to the show. But then, mine did, too. She's a damn fine-looking woman."

Seth sipped away with that Mona Lisa smile.

Travis tore off his bill cap and scrubbed his hair. "Dad and *Nancy?*" The thought was jarring.

After so many years of seeing his father steer clear of serious relationships, he'd assumed no woman would ever replace their mother.

He resettled his cap. "Hell, I didn't think Dad was *horny,* I thought he was lonely. He's been acting kind of down, now that Jake's moved to an apartment and we're all so busy...." The truth smacked Travis upside the head with stunning force. *Well, whaddaya know.*

"What is it?" Cameron said sharply.

"Seth's right. Dad hasn't been acting lonely. He's been acting lovesick."

Seth broke into his rare full-blown crooked Malloy grin.

Jake soon joined him, then Cameron, and finally, Travis, who couldn't believe he'd been so rock-dumb.

The curvy waitress approached their table with her head down, her gaze on the check she carried. She appeared to be making sure the total was accurate. "Can I get you boys anything else?"

"No, we're about ready to pop," Jake said.

She looked up and around at the full barrage of grins, her expression dazed.

"We've got something to celebrate," Jake told the woman he'd flirted with at length. "Heard anything about that new club on the Richmond strip? Night Fever, I think it's called."

Gravity tugged hard at Travis's mouth.

"Um...Martha?" Jake prodded.

She started, flushed and slapped down the check. "Sorry. Night Fever? Yeah, if you like retro disco music, you'll love it. It's not very far from here, either."

Travis groaned.

"Thursday is ladies' night," she added.

Jake grinned wider and looked at Travis.

"Over your dead body."

Jake looked at Cameron.

"Still want a Viking funeral?"

Jake looked at Seth.

"No."

Turning back to Martha, the son of a bitch wrapped an arm around her plump waist and raised the long-lashed little-boy eyes few women could resist. "So, heading north on Richmond, would the club be after, or before Fondren?"

"HERE WE GO, doll. This is perfect," Vinnie said above the background throb of music.

The club, appropriately named Night Fever, was surprisingly crowded for Thursday night. He'd by-passed the tables filled with couples and clusters of women to reach this half-moon cozy booth. It faced, not the dance floor, but the line of mostly male customers lounging against a long bar.

Lisa had been right about him wanting other men to see the Mystery Woman draped over his arm.

Prodded by the pain of three chunky gold rings digging into her lower back, Kara slipped into the booth, then scooted around as far as she could.

Instead of following, Vinnie cocked his ear as if entranced with the Bee Gees song "Staying Alive," then turned toward the dance floor. Night Fever's ambiance replicated that of the club John Travolta's character had favored in *Saturday Night Fever*.

The dance floor, lit from underneath, changed colors periodically. Mirror-tiled balls hung from the ceiling, spraying shards of light over the crowd. And the music was equally awful. Pure disco. Kara had little interest in rediscovering bad taste.

But during the seventies, Vinnie would've been a young Italian stallion just starting to feel—and sow—his oats. The concierge at his hotel had told him about Night Fever, and Vinnie had suggested coming here after dinner.

This was his fantasy, so she'd feigned enthusiasm to relive his youth.

He'd probably been quite the stud minus his receding hairline and slight paunch. Not that he wasn't attractive now. He was. In a balding paunchy Itallion stallion kinda way. She found herself studying him with more fondness than she would've thought possible only hours ago.

His dark suit was fashionable, the quality excellent, the fit flawless over his stocky frame. He'd ditched his tie and unbuttoned his shirt to below the throat. Nestled on a wedge of black chest hair, a thick gold chain gleamed in the dim light.

To her horror, his hips began a subdued bump and grind to the beat of the song. Any minute now, he would point his finger to the sky Travolta-style.

"Vinnie?"

He turned. "Yeah, babe?"

"I'm a little thirsty," she said in her best Mystery Woman sex-kitten voice.

"Okay, babe, me too. I gotta go leak the dog anyway, so I'll stop by the bar first, and leave our drink orders. What's your pleasure?"

She shook off the extremely unwelcome image he'd conjured. "Um…Perrier with a twist."

His expression fell. "Not even a glass of wine?"

She'd had two at Tony's restaurant and would have to drive herself home. "I wish I could, but I have an early photo session. Alcohol dehydrates my skin." She looked up coyly through her lashes. "And the Valentine collection shows a lot of skin."

His black eyes assumed an unfocused glaze as he obviously envisioned the collection.

He was so easily manipulated by the illusion she'd created that her initial thrill of power had long since faded. She waited impatiently for him to resurface.

"Vinnie, our drinks?"

His gaze sharpened.

Careful. Mustn't sound too much like the Kara he knows. She licked her lips, and his eyes followed the movement. "I'm just so thirsty."

"Oh. Yeah. Now you stay put, babe. And tell any jerk who comes over here while I'm gone that you're with me." For a moment, he seemed torn between the desire to guard his territory and an equally basic urgent need. The call of nature won. "I'll be back in a jiff."

She watched him walk to the bar and shoulder his way close enough to place an order. When he turned to check on her, she wiggled her fingers.

His chest expanded. He swept a crowing gaze over the stag line, then strutted off to the restroom.

Shaking her head, Kara untied the cashmere shawl knotted loosely above her breasts. The luxurious wool had kept her warm on the drive here from the restaurant. Yes, the Miata was a tight squeeze, but once inside with the seat moved back all the way, she hadn't felt ridiculous. She'd felt dashing and adventurous and young.

She dropped the shawl over her clutch purse and lifted a hand to her hair. Hopelessly windblown. In the ladies room at Tony's she'd tamed the wild tousle upon arrival. She almost reached for her purse and comb now.

The Mystery Woman lowered her hand to her lap.

Bedroom hair fit her role. Vinnie mustn't learn who she was, or he'd feel foolish and manipulated. He might retract his discounted printing price. Worse, he might reveal the Mystery Woman's identity to others, the secret trickling to the wrong ears, as secrets always do. Ross was touting Kara in station promos as "the voice of today's woman." She somehow doubted today's liberated woman wanted a lingerie model representing her thoughts and feelings. And if Gram found out....

Shuddering, Kara vowed that Vinnie would have no cause to question her legitimacy. He'd get the full fantasy for his loss of profit printing the catalogs. She never welshed on a deal. Her business integrity was inviolate.

Even if she had discovered a distressing ability to lie through her teeth about her personal life.

At dinner, she'd refused to give Vinnie a name or telephone number, saying her Mystery Woman contract specified absolute secrecy. He'd called her ''babe'' and ''doll'' willingly enough, but had wanted to pursue a relationship beyond one date. To discourage that line of thinking, she'd invented Dirk: a tall, blond, handsome and extremely jealous fiancé. If Dirk knew she was out with another man tonight, he would kill her and Vinnie both.

Vinnie might be a little crude, but he wasn't the least bit stupid. He'd stopped talking about future liaisons.

Wondering what was taking him so long, Kara glanced toward the restrooms—and blinked. Over half the men leaning against the bar were staring at her. A few ogled her pearl pendant. But the rest...well, didn't. Yet they seemed intrigued, a little dazed and a lot admiring.

To those men, she flashed a startled, but genuine Kara, smile.

It was like watching a bank of arc lights switch on to see them smile in return. Amazing. She basked in their obvious delight.

If they weren't responding to Mystery Woman's body, to what, then? To her smile? To an expression that wasn't embarrassed or giving off I'm-not-interested signals? Her smile warmed at the thought.

The oglers stopped leering and broke into smiles.

She laughed out loud. This was ten times headier than the power she'd exerted over Vinnie. He thought she was sexy.

They thought she was nice.

Vinnie walked into view, glaring at the beaming stag line as he bellied up to the bar and paid for their drinks. Her admirers quickly found something else to admire.

Okay, Kara conceded. Her…pearl might've scored her some personality points with those men. But the experience had opened her eyes. When she returned to being a lady, she would try not to confuse unfriendliness or insecurity with modesty.

The lights suddenly dimmed and the music slowed. She didn't recognize the song, but it was tolerably pleasant.

Vinnie approached the booth carrying two squat glasses before him like an offering to the gods. Kara slid around the seat and stood.

Dismay widened his eyes, exposing a flicker of insecurity. Men were people, too.

"Are you leaving?"

"Yes." She took the drinks from his resistant grip, set his glass on the table and sipped from hers thirstily.

"But...where are you going?"

Finishing her water, Kara clunked down the glass. "To the dance floor—" she grabbed his hand "—with you."

They joined the stream of couples fast filling every square inch of the rectangular floor. Men who wouldn't risk embarrassing themselves during a lively song were more than willing to lock bodies with a woman and sway from foot to foot. She claimed a spot in one corner, and he gathered her into a clinch.

"Man, I can't believe I'm holdin' you like this. Wait till the guys back at the shop hear about—"

"Vinnie?"

"Yeah, babe?"

"If I hear another word about the guys back at the shop, I really will leave the club."

"Oh. Okay. Sorry."

He pressed her closer and kept silent, spinning God knew what fantasy in his mind. This was one case where ignorance was definitely bliss. Besides, she could hardly point fingers.

In the dark, in the swaying crowd, in the arms of

the wrong man, Kara spun her own fantasy, replacing Vinnie with the man she wanted—right or wrong.

The music ended. The lights came up. The next selection would be lively.

Men scurried for cover like roaches. All but about five great dancers and their partners remained.

And Vinnie.

As the Bee Gees song "More Than a Woman" commenced, he looked at her so hopefully, she didn't have the heart to ruin his trip down memory lane and drag him off. So she began dancing. And for the first time, he smiled as if he thought she was nice, not sexy.

Ruthlessly squelching the urge to confirm they were the object of derision, she focused only on Vinnie. His arms pumping, his pelvis bumping, his bald spot already beginning to sweat, he was groovin' out and having the time of his life. What was the crime in that? She loosened up.

Before long, she was even having fun. When he pointed to the sky, she mimicked his movement, but she let him do a duck walk across the floor alone. By the time the song ended, she'd laughed so hard her stomach hurt. Whew! She needed to rest.

Pulling him off the dance floor, she heard a smattering of applause and a few whistles. Oh, thank goodness she'd let Vinnie have his moment in the spotlight. From the expression on his face, his fantasy was complete.

Everywhere she looked people were smiling. That group of five women on the left. Those two couples on the right. The four men blocking their path...weren't smiling. They appeared stunned.

Kara stopped. The blood drained from her face.

Her mind struggled in the absence of oxygen to think of a way to circumvent disaster.

Jake recovered first and started grinning. Seth and Cameron showed signs the shock was wearing off. Any second, one of them would blurt her name.

"Hey, babe, what's the problem? Do you know these guys?"

CHAPTER THIRTEEN

GOOD LORD! That was Kara walking toward him smiling at the crowd, her eyes sparkling with pleasure, her hair a sexy mess, her complexion as flushed and dewy as if she'd just left her lover's bed instead of the dance floor. Her cream-colored skirt and top were so tight she looked dipped in white chocolate. A mouth-watering temptation drawing every masculine eye in the room.

Gaping at the blond creature depriving him of oxygen, Travis suddenly empathized with the fish he yanked from safe waters into an alien world. Due to "catch and release" regulations, the shock to their primitive nervous systems was temporary.

He wasn't sure his highly advanced sensory neurons would recover.

What in *hell* was she doing in a meat market like this dressed like a decadent dessert? The balding joker with her didn't look capable of warding off possible trouble.

Then again, trouble would have to get past all four Malloys first. No small challenge. Travis glanced at his brothers for reassurance—and scowled. Jake, Seth and Cameron appeared to have developed a raging sweet tooth.

"Hey, babe, what's the problem? Do you know these guys?"

Travis's narrowed gaze shot to Disco Man, whose swarthy hand rested too damn close to a delectable tush. As for Kara…

Her rosy flush had bleached chalk-white. The look she swept over each brother in turn held panic and a silent plea.

"Dirk!" she cried, lunging straight toward Cameron. She fell against his chest and twined her arms around his neck.

He stared down in obvious bemusement. "Hi, K—"

Her mouth cut off his reply.

As Travis's incredulity and blood pressure skyrocketed, Cameron seemed to unfreeze. His limp embrace tightened, his hands slid near a curvy backside, his head angled as if to deepen the kiss.

Kara broke the connection abruptly and stepped away from him, her complexion a bright pink. "Don't be mad, sugar, I can explain." She turned to the stocky man eyeing Cameron nervously. "Vinnie is a business acquaintance, not my date. Please don't hurt him!"

Cameron's gaze smoldered, all right, but not with anger. For an ugly instant, Travis wanted to smash his fist in his brother's too handsome face.

"Why don't we go outside where it's quieter?" Kara suggested. "Vinnie, could you come with us, please?"

Looking a little green around the gills, Vinnie nodded.

"Thank you." Smiling weakly, she focused on Jake and Seth, who only needed bags of popcorn to complete the picture they made. "There's no need to ruin y'all's fun. Stay here and enjoy yourselves. Dirk can fill you in later...right, sugar?" Moving toward Cameron, she stretched out her hand.

He stepped forward smoothly and grasped slim white fingers. "Whatever you say, honey."

What in *hell* was Kara's game?

Without so much as a glance in Travis's direction, she pulled the cosmopolitan brother of choice deeper into the club. Vinnie trailed obediently behind. The grin Cameron flashed over his shoulder was more than a little smug.

Travis started to move, only to find himself gripped on each arm and held in place.

"Take it easy, bro," Jake said from the left.

"Yeah, he's only trying to help Kara out of whatever jam she's in," Seth spoke from the right.

Travis craned his neck to keep the trio in his line of vision. They veered to a booth near the bar, where Kara scooped up her purse and a bundle of white material, then continued toward the club entrance. Taking a deep breath, Travis forced himself to relax. The manacles on his arms loosened.

He surged forward and free of restraint.

Dodging people and tables, he kept his quarry in sight. They made a striking pair, Dirk and the babe did. As perfectly matched as the newlyweds framed above the fireplace at Taylor House. Heads turned as the beautiful blond couple passed, adding fuel to the hurt and jealousy burning a hole in Travis's gut. Emotions a distant part of him said were unjustified.

The in-your-face part wasn't listening.

Ahead, the club's hammered brass door opened to admit a cluster of young women. Cameron, Kara and Vinnie slipped outside before the door eased shut.

Travis swerved around a startled brunette, bumped chests with a giggling redhead and rebounded into a squealing blonde. By the time he pushed through the front door into the crisp night air, his muscles were knotted again.

He paused to get his bearings and spotted a silver-blond head at the edge of the club's well-lit parking lot. Travis headed for Kara, intent on getting to the bottom of her charade, just as Jake and Seth burst outside.

Fortunately her back was turned as they approached.

"...You know how demanding she can be," Kara was saying. "Vinnie is printing her catalogs, and he wanted to meet me. I owed Kara this favor. But I swear, Dirk, there's no reason to be jealous.''

Cameron didn't bat an eyelash at his brothers, but Vinnie cast uneasy glances over Kara's shoulder.

''Vinnie is flying home to New York tomorrow. He doesn't expect to see me again—'' She broke off and spun around, targeting her peeved glare at Travis. ''Do you mind? This is a private conversation.''

Travis might've laughed at her breathy bimbo voice if it hadn't whispered over his libido, hardening more than his resolve. Self-disgust joined his other combustible emotions, the whole intolerable mixture converting to welcome anger.

He looked at Vinnie. ''You got any objection to me hearing this?''

The New Yorker shrank back a half step, then raised placating palms. ''No, man, it's cool. But all I did was dance with your girlfriend—'' his dark eyes skittered to Cameron ''—I mean, Dirk's fiancée—'' he glanced uncertainly at Jake and Seth ''—I mean, the Mystery Woman model. Not to worry. She never even told me her name or gave me her phone number. Even if I wanted to—which I don't—I couldn't contact her or leak her secret.''

Mystery woman? Secret? What in hell was going on?

''Jeez Louise,'' Jake murmured in an awed tone,

gazing at Kara as if he was about to fall on his knees and bow.

She smiled at Vinnie gently. "I'm going to call it a night, but there are a lot of women inside who need dance partners. Why don't you stay?"

He hitched back his coat sleeve and checked his watch. "Yeah, maybe I will. That is…if you're sure you'll be okay with these guys."

Despite the sheen of sweat at his receding hairline, his squared shoulders and jaw raised him a notch in Travis's estimation.

Cameron moved close to Kara and put an arm possessively around her waist. "Don't worry. She's in good hands."

"I'll be fine, Vinnie," Kara seconded. "Now get back in there and give those women a treat."

"Okay, doll. But it won't be near as much fun." With a parting wistful smile for Kara, he turned and hurried off toward the club's entrance.

The group watched silently until he went inside, releasing a blast of music quickly muffled by the closing door.

A cold breeze stirred and Kara shivered, her full body shimmy raising Travis's temperature another few degrees.

In a blink, Cameron had unwrapped the folded white material she clutched and gallantly draped the shawl—and his arm—around her shoulders. He was just Sir friggin' Lancelot tonight.

"Thank you, Cameron," she said in her normal voice, giving him a dazzling smile. "For everything. You really came through for me earlier. But I apologize for putting you in such an awkward position."

"Are you kidding? That's one of the most enjoyable positions I've ever been in. But, hey, if you thought it was awkward, I'm more than willing to practice until we get it right." His wolfish grin left no doubt he referred to their kiss.

"Just tell me when," he added, clearly only half teasing.

In answer, she slipped out from under his arm and gave it an affectionate pat.

"Does that mean no?" Cameron tugged one end of her shawl. "You're breakin' my heart—"

"Cut the crap, Cameron!" Travis instantly felt better. Ready and eager to rumble.

Tawny eyes lifted to study him mildly. Travis wasn't fooled.

"Or what, big brother?"

"Or I'll kick the crap out of you."

The mouth Kara had kissed hardened. "In your dreams."

"Later, maybe. First, I'll kick your ass for real. Unless you're too chicken?"

The challenge hovered between them. Someone—Seth?—muttered a disgusted curse.

Genuine anger sparked in Cameron's eyes. "You name the place and time, old man."

"What's wrong with here and now?"

"Fine!"

"Good!"

Travis and Cam moved forward simultaneously.

Seth stepped between the two, extending his arms like a referee. "Calm down, you idiots, or I'll kick both your asses! Travis, if you're so crazy jealous you'll fight your own brother over Kara, you might want to pay attention when she walks away. She's half-way across the parking lot now."

Travis blinked. "Huh?"

"Damn, Travis," Jake blurted. "Why didn't you tell us Kara was the Mystery Woman?"

"Huh?"

He peered closer at Travis, then did the same to Seth and Cameron. "Oh, man, none of you knows what I'm talking about, do you? God, do you all live on Planet Clueless? *Mystery Woman* is a hot new lingerie catalog that never shows the model's face. And the model is Kara! She didn't want Vinnie to know her real identity." Jake stared at Travis with more respect than he'd displayed since grade school. "Jeez, bro. You've slept with a goddess."

"The goddess is about to take off in a little red convertible," Seth observed dryly.

Travis whirled around and searched the parking lot. A movement caught his eye, and sure enough, there was Kara driving a red Miata, backing out of a space. She'd put him through hell tonight and revealed a secret life that deserved a full explanation. And what was she doing?

Running away.

Again.

He watched her shift gears, heard tires squeal as the Miata jerked forward, experienced a surge of tumultuous anger as she zipped toward the exit, looking damn good in the little car she'd supposedly refused to ride in.

Without making a conscious decision, he loped forward, digging keys from his pocket on the way to his Jeep.

"I hope she kicks the crap out of you," Cameron yelled behind him.

If she did, it wouldn't be the first time, Travis thought grimly. But *this* time, he intended to get some answers, too.

As KARA pulled into the town house's one-car garage, she congratulated herself on a clean getaway. Leaving without saying goodbye or answering more questions would catch up to her all too soon. For tonight, at least, she'd bought herself time to recover from the emotional wringer of masquerading as the Mystery Woman.

Sighing, she switched off the ignition and opened the convertible's door. Getting out of the Miata was a bit tricky, but she loved this little car! Lisa was right. It was great fun to drive with the top down. Standing, Kara smoothed her hopelessly tangled hair before leaning in to gather her purse and shawl. She'd just slammed the door when the overhead garage door opener light blinked off.

Great. She'd put the remote control back in her purse. Popping open the clasp, she fumbled for and found the button, then pressed.

Overhead, the mechanical pulley whirred into action. The automatic light switched on. She took a step forward—and shrieked as a man ducked beneath the lowering garage door.

Travis slowly straightened, his dark eyes glinting beneath the bill of a Lake Kimberly ball cap.

The door clunked to a stop.

Lifting a palm from her wildly pounding heart, Kara narrowed her eyes. "You scared the life out of me!"

"Serves you right. You should've hit that remote button the second you pulled in. But then, you're living dangerously tonight, aren't you...babe?"

Uh-oh. So much for buying time. "You're the one taking stupid chances. You must've driven like a madman to get here so fast. And what if I'd had a gun just now, Travis? I could've shot you."

"Have you started packing a gun on top of everything else, Kara? What other nasty little secrets are you hiding?"

His mood hadn't improved since she'd left him flexing his muscles at Cameron. "Look, you're obviously spoiling for a fight, but I'm too tired to oblige. I want a hot bath and a good night's sleep. Take two aspirin and call me in the morning when your jockstrap's not in a bunch, okay?"

Big mistake.

He suddenly seemed to fill the garage, and he hadn't even moved. The door leading to Lisa's town house was opposite the passenger side of the car. Kara glanced at the front bumper too close to the wall for her to squeeze through. Her only route of escape was past Travis.

"I'm sorry," she said, meaning it. He looked edgy, restless and very dangerous. "I shouldn't have said that."

"Give the girl a gold star."

"You want to know what tonight was all about? Fine. I'll tell you." Anything to make him leave. "I needed to bring in cash for Taylor Fine Foundations. Lisa and I came up with the concept for a direct mail lingerie catalog called *Mystery Woman*. It's taken off in a big way.

"Vinnie's shop in New York prints the catalogs. He agreed to discount the next huge print run if I got him a date with the model. Me. Except...he didn't know it was me. The model's face never shows in the photographs, and he and I had only talked on the phone. So I dressed like this—" she switched to her sex kitten voice "—and talked like this, and he swallowed the story, hook, line and sinker."

"He looked ready to jump in the damn boat."

She stiffened beneath his thorough appraisal, ignoring tendrils of warmth wherever his gaze lingered.

"Not that I blame the guy, with you dressed like that. I never figured you for a tease, Kara. You're lucky Jake dragged the rest of us into that club."

Outrage swept away any trace of guilt. "I *never* led Vinnie on. Dinner and dancing. That's all I offered. And when he pressured me for more, I handled the situation."

Travis's gaze came up, glittering with menace. "He pressured you?"

Startled, she chose her next words carefully. "Only in a nice way. The point is, contrary to what you think, I don't need rescuing anymore, Travis. I'd already invented a jealous fiancé named Dirk who kept Vinnie in line. Then you and the rest of the Cartwright brothers swaggered into the saloon. I knew that one of you would blow my cover or try to protect the little lady, unless I acted fast."

"You acted fast, all right. More like a saloon whore than a little lady."

Pain ripped through her body, robbing her of speech. She mentally groped for—and found—a strengthening dose of Taylor pride.

Lifting her chin, she said with quiet dignity, "I'd like you to leave now, please."

Travis looked down at the floor and uttered a succinct curse. The bill of his cap shielded his expression, but the muscular shoulders under his white T-shirt were rigid, the bronzed arms at his sides corded with tension. When his head lifted, she braced herself for more abuse.

The torment darkening his eyes sent another jolt to her toes—this one of surprise.

"I'm sorry, Kara. I haven't been jealous of Cameron in twenty years. Women are drawn to his flashy looks like bass to a school of shiners. He can't help it. Seth and Jake and I used to tease him about it, and envy him a little, until his revolving-door girlfriends started seeming more like a curse than a blessing. But tonight…when you threw yourself in his arms…"

She stared in amazement at the long fingers curling into fists.

"When you kissed Cam instead of me…I wanted to tear off his pretty face with my bare hands. My own *brother,* for cripe's sake! I've got no excuse for calling you a—well, what I called you a minute ago, except that you're making me goddamn *crazy* in that tight little number you're wearing."

No woman alive could remain unaffected by such a confession. Shivering through a dark thrill, Kara struggled to focus on his pain. "Travis, when I told

Vinnie about my fiancé, I described him as being blond. Last time I looked, only one of the Malloy brothers was blond. *That's* why I kissed Cam. No other reason.''

The moment stretched.

Separated from him by about ten feet, Kara sensed the molecules of anger and hurt between them evolving, becoming sexually charged and crackling with energy. His eyes took on a golden gleam.

''So what are you saying, Kara? That you would've kissed me if you'd had a choice?''

The balance of power had shifted, and he relished the change, damn him!

He walked forward slowly, eliminating more oxygen the closer he drew. An arm's length away, he stopped.

''Talk to me, Kara. Would you have chosen me?''

His eyes challenged her to cross a line she hadn't stepped over in nine years. Resentment and helpless desire swelled within Kara.

The safest answer was no answer. Watching his hand reach out, she thought he must surely hear the heartbeat thundering in her chest.

He removed the purse and shawl from her lifeless grip and tossed them onto the trunk of the car. ''Don't feel like talking? No problem.''

She stared up into the burning eyes of a tiger.

"Show me," he ordered.

The overhead light winked out.

Kara blinked. With the garage door closed, only a faint glow from the street lamps shone through a row of small windowpanes. She saw Travis only as a looming shadow.

But heat emanated from his body in tangible waves. The scent of crisp cologne and warm skin and mesquite smoke teased her nose. She could hear him breathing faster than normal, almost as if he were winded. As if he weren't the undisputed Sibling King, superbly fit and able to kick the crap out of all opponents.

Show him?

She should run like hell in the opposite direction.

"Show me…please."

The gruff entreaty handed equal power to Kara, liberating emotions and needs too long held in check. She lifted her arms, twined them around his neck and raised on tiptoe, her mouth searching for his.

At first contact, her lips trembled, then clung tentatively, then pressed joyfully.

Dear God, yes! This was the right brother. The brother she'd wanted to kiss. The one who drew her like a bass to shiners—not with flash—but with rugged masculinity. She nudged the seam of his lips with her tongue, gained entrance to his mouth and proceeded to show him he was her first choice.

Her only choice.

Everything about him aroused her, and she wasn't the shy girl he'd married. She knew what she wanted and she took it, tasting him boldly, tugging the shirt from his jeans to touch hot skin and contoured muscles. Rubbing against the hard ridge pressing into her belly. Striving to position him properly, where the pleasure was greatest. If only she'd worn heels!

It had been so long. She'd missed him so much. A thousand nights she'd yearned for what he'd taught her to crave. A sound of pure frustration tore from her throat.

Rumbling deep in his chest, Travis turned her shoulders and walked swiftly backward to bump against the car. With her body stabilized, he took over the kiss. His clever tongue swirled and stroked, his knees dipping to place him where they both wanted. He thrust his hips.

She bit his lip.

The kiss turned wild.

She'd never felt passion like this, not even in their lust-filled honeymoon days. Liquid fire seared her veins and melted her bones, incinerating her caution. She reached between them and relearned the shape and size and heat of him, exulting in his indrawn hiss.

Strong hands suddenly gripped her waist, hitched her onto the low trunk and spread her knees. She opened them shamelessly wider as Travis moved closer, never breaking the kiss. One exploratory palm slid over her thigh-high stocking and met the skin above.

He went completely still.

Then he ripped his mouth away, leaned his forehead against hers and released a long tortured groan.

He was stopping?

Kara tried to recapture his lips, but he turned his head.

Was he really *stopping?*

"Travis, please," she choked out, beyond pride.

"I don't have any protection with me," he said thickly. "You don't happen to have anything in your purse, do you?"

She should have been insulted. Instead, she felt like crying. Every part of her pulsed in regret. "No."

His chest still rose and fell like bellows. She caught her breath as his hand slid slowly up her thigh. Yes!

His lips nibbled her ear, her jaw, her—

Light flooded the garage.

Travis jerked back and closed her knees.

Dazed, her lips stinging and burning, Kara twisted toward the side door.

"Oops!" Lisa exclaimed, one hand on the light switch, the other clutching a tennis racket. "I was half asleep and thought I heard a shriek. I started worrying and had to check it out. But I can see you're okay.''

Not hardly.

"Lisa, wait!'' The reality of what she'd almost done struck her hard. Kara gathered her purse and shawl and slid off the hood. "I'll walk back to the house with you.''

Avoiding Travis's stare, she did what she should have done much earlier.

She ran like hell.

KARA AWAKENED by slow degrees to light that was too bright for a west exposure, the whirring sound of a blender Taylor House didn't possess, the delicious smell of bacon Gram didn't like. Groggy and disoriented, she opened her eyes fully. Taupe wall. Matching accordion window shade. Eggshell carpet. Lisa's guest bedroom.

Turning on her back, Kara realized she clutched a pillow between her thighs and released a long moan of humiliation.

How could she look Travis in the eye now that he knew her deepest secret? Not her clandestine modeling and direct-marketing activities. But the fact that she still burned for him.

She moaned again.

"Quit thinking about last night and come eat breakfast,'' Lisa called from the kitchen.

The thought of eating suddenly made Kara nauseous, but she flipped back the covers. Replaying that kiss over and over would make her crazy. She slipped out of bed, made a pit stop to take care of business and splash water on her face, then headed for the kitchen and sympathy.

Lisa lifted her gaze from the skillet of scrambled eggs she was stirring. "You look like something the cat dragged in."

Such a comfort, Lisa was.

"I feel worse," Kara admitted, perching on one of four stools surrounding a granite-topped island counter. She toyed with her place setting. "I always thought problems were supposed to seem less burdensome in the morning."

"Nah. That's just a platitude people tell people with problems so everyone can get some sleep."

Always there for her, Lisa was, through thick and thin.

Beside the range top, two plates held three strips of bacon each. "Thanks for making breakfast. But I really don't think I can eat."

"Oh, good! I'm starving, and I only scrambled four eggs." Lisa lifted the skillet and scraped the entire fluffy mass onto her plate, then snatched the extra bacon as well. She carried her loaded plate to the island and settled on a stool. "There's coffee on the warmer and frozen orange juice in the blender. Would you pour me some juice while you're up?''

Yep, true-blue and unselfish, that was Lisa.

Kara had filled the first glass with juice and was starting on the second when the wall phone rang.

Lisa kept right on eating.

"Don't bother getting up," Kara said wryly. "I'll get it." She freed her hands, moved to the phone and lifted the receiver. "Hello?"

"Lisa, this is Major McKinney. May I speak with Kara, please?" Where was the authoritarian boom in his voice? He sounded old. And scared.

Oh God, oh God. "Major? This is Kara speaking. Is something wrong?"

"Now, don't panic, Kara, but your grandmother is in the emergency room at Methodist Hospital."

"What?" Her gaze flew to Lisa, who'd stopped chewing and watched intently.

"It's her heart. They've got her stabilized now, but she needs surgery. You need to get here as soon as you can and sign the release form."

Kara swayed and reached out blindly. A chair scraped back. And then small hands were gripping her fingers, giving her strength.

"Kara?" the Major prodded. "Can you do that, honey?"

"Yes," she whispered. "What happened?"

"Something…upset her and she went into cardiac arrest. I'll tell you everything when you get here. Do you think you can get Lisa to drive you here?''

''Yes,'' Kara said unhesitatingly of her true-blue unselfish friend.

''That's good. Does she know which hospital it is? The medical center can be pretty confusing.''

Without a word, Kara transferred the receiver to her friend.

She heard little of the ensuing one-way conversation. The earth had opened up beneath her feet, and she lay whimpering at the bottom of a black frightening hole. One thought, originating from that place where intuition dwelled, pummeled her brain into cowering submission.

My fault—my fault—my fault—my fault…

CHAPTER FOURTEEN

THE WAITING nearly broke Kara.

Despite knowing the coronary artery bypass surgery would take a minimum of five hours, she refused to budge from the small seating area designated for families and close friends. Nurse Bradley had said Dr. Sloan would come here directly from surgery to report Gram's condition. What if he finished early and Kara was in the cafeteria or roaming the halls?

No, here he would come, and here she would sit. A growling stomach, raging thirst and stiffening muscles were small penance to pay for her sins.

She flipped blindly through her fifth magazine, unable to focus on print or even the television mounted high in one corner. Major McKinney sat in a nearby chair. Lisa had left to make phone calls. Margaret, whose husband was having a cancerous brain tumor removed, sat on a sofa pretending to watch *The Price Is Right*. Kara had bonded instantly with the stranger through shared anxiety for a loved one. The poor woman had a longer wait ahead of her than Kara.

Sighing, she flung her magazine on an empty chair. If the doctors had let her, she would gladly have donated her heart to replace her grandmother's damaged organ. After all, it was her deceit that had caused Gram's cardiac arrest.

My fault—my fault—my fault.

Kara leaned forward, propped her elbows on her knees and buried her face in her palms.

"She'll be fine," Major McKinney said in a hearty voice. "You'll see."

Kara nodded without lifting her head.

Thank God he'd been with Gram earlier. He'd called 911 and continued CPR until the ambulance arrived. The emergency medic team credited him with preventing brain damage. For that, Kara could never repay him.

It remained to be seen whether the skilled surgical team would save her grandmother's life for the second time that day.

Regret and guilt slumped her shoulders. She should have known about the pain Dr. Sloan said Gram must have been experiencing for some time. Kara should have taken her grandmother for a checkup, rather than assume a woman who hated such things would follow through. Most of all, she'd been a coward to try and hide her *Mystery Woman* endeavor, and naive to think she could.

Why hadn't she revealed her direct-marketing activities months ago? She could have explained her reasons and softened the impact.

Instead, she'd left Gram vulnerable to shocking perfidy.

Major McKinney had seen the newspaper lying on the front porch when he'd brought over banana muffins to share with Gram. An envelope had been taped to the outer plastic wrapping. He'd innocently handed the odd delivery to her after she opened the door. The Major had apologized to Kara for that.

Apologized. To *her.* Oh, she couldn't bear it.

Compelled by a need Kara knew was unhealthy, but which she was helpless to control, she lifted her head, reached for her purse and pulled out an envelope. Ignoring the Major's faint sound of distress, she withdrew the folded letter and opened it to reread.

Dear Esther,

How I wish I could watch your expression when you see the *Houston Express*'s front-page photo of your fine upstanding granddaughter. That's her, you know, wearing that red corselette and fishnet stockings, even though you can't see her face. She enjoys showing off her body to men as much as Pamela did. Maybe more. Your precious Kara is nothing but a trashy slut. And now everyone in Houston will know it.

I timed things perfectly, if I do say so. The talk-show co-host that the *Houston Chronicle* called "the voice of the new-millennium woman" in yesterday's newspaper, has a front-page headline today. A little dramatic, but that's exactly why I gave the story to the *Houston Express.*

"One Small Step for Woman, One Giant Leap Back for Womankind."

Are you getting the whole dirty picture yet, Esther? Everyone else will, when they open their mailboxes and pull out a *Mystery Woman* catalog. They'll get an eyeful of Kara on every page, wearing the sleazy lingerie you won't let her sell at Taylor Fine Foundations. When the news about Kara's dirty little side business spreads, the Taylor name will be an even bigger joke than it is now. I suppose she'll get fired from her hot-shot television show, too.

Poor Kara. Poor Esther. How humiliating for you both. You might even be experiencing a fraction of the pain I felt when Pamela stole my life, my heart, my one true love. He loved me first, and she couldn't stand that. So she led him into temptation, and delivered him an evil child, born of sin—not love. After she dumped him, he was too ashamed to return to me.

At last I have, if not peace, a justice of sorts.

Your devoted employee,
Carol

P.S. Oh, by the way, I quit. Don't bother trying
to find me or taking legal action. The moment
Kara became a "celebrity," every detail of her
life became "news," not an invasion of privacy.

Kara slowly refolded the letter, slipped it back
into the envelope and dropped the missive into her
purse. Her fingers trembled from contact with the
writer's terrible malice. She'd known Carol was a
bitter, unhappy woman, and certainly unpleasant.
But her actions spoke of true mental instability.
When Kara thought of all the hate and meticulous
planning that had culminated in her grandmother's
collapse, she shuddered.

And buried the kernel of information that at least
one person in the world knew the identity of her
father.

Across the room, Margaret had stretched out on
the couch. Suddenly the emotional night and trau-
matic morning caught up with Kara. She was so
very tired. Leaning back, she rested her head
against the wall, her eyelids sliding shut. Immediately a vision of her grandmother reading the article, then clutching her chest, filled her with horror.

This time her moan escaped.

Seconds later a tentative hand patted her shoulder. "There, there, Esther's a strong-willed woman. Dr. Sloan is one of the finest cardio-thoracic surgeons in the country. Your grandmother will come through like a trouper."

Kara lifted her head and met the Major's worried eyes. "If she does, it's no thanks to me."

He frowned. "You mustn't blame yourself."

"No? Who should I blame? Carol? She leaked the story, but I provided the juicy news in the first place. Should I blame Gram's heart? It was performing just fine until I shamed it into stopping."

He cleared his throat uncomfortably. "You're being far too harsh on yourself."

She shook her head miserably. "I'm being—"

"*Melodramatic,* is the word," a feminine voice interrupted firmly. "My, my. You can *shame* a heart into stopping?"

Kara twisted around. She'd never been so glad to see anyone in her life.

Lisa arched a brow. "What can you do for an encore, Kara? Embarrass a kidney into renal failure?"

She swept into the room, delivering sarcasm, two McDonald's bags and a fierce hug in that order.

"Eat," she commanded, sitting beside Kara so that she was sandwiched between staunch support. "The Breakfast Jack is yours. Major, I brought you a Big Mac, since you skipped your banana muffin this morning. Cokes for everyone. And one of those orders of fries has my name one it. Any word from the doctor?''

Bless Lisa and her practicality.

Kara let the Major handle conversation a while and applied herself to the business of refueling. In short order, she'd demolished her sandwich, every last fry and half her drink. Sighing, she bagged her trash and experienced a marginal lift in spirits.

''I called everyone on the list,'' Lisa said between bites of French fry. ''Mr. Decker at Holiday Cleaners said Carol never opened the store this morning. He'll put a Temporarily Closed sign on the front door until you can get over there and check to see what that spawn of the devil might've ripped off. I didn't tell *him* that, of course.'' She took a sip of Coke. ''I hope she stole you blind, so we can put her ass in jail—sorry, Major.''

''My sentiments, exactly,'' he boomed.

''Did you talk directly to Ross?'' Kara's French fries turned ugly on her. She shouldn't have let her friend do her dirty work.

''Yes.'' Lisa's expression softened. ''He asked me a million questions about Esther. She's his first concern. He hadn't read or heard about the *Houston Express* article yet. But he said to tell you not to worry. He'd come up with a damage-control plan. He was really wonderful about the whole thing, Kara.''

''You sound surprised.''

"You're not?"

Kara examined her feelings. At some point during the course of their business association, Ross had become a friend. "No. I was concerned about jeopardizing his career, not about him going ballistic."

Lisa sipped her drink thoughtfully. Popped another fry in her mouth.

Kara stood it as long as she could. "Did you call Travis?"

Dark eyes widened. "Oh, hon, I'm sorry. Of course I called, but I talked to Nancy. He took a client out fishing at dawn. She said she'd call his cell phone, but that half the time he forgets to leave it on. I didn't go into any details with Nancy about the catalog, or anything."

"Like it's a big secret now."

Kara listened glumly as Lisa recited the reactions of a handful of Gram's friends. Their love and prayers were welcome, but Kara felt oddly bereft. Only this morning she hadn't known how she would face Travis, and now all she wanted was to see him.

It made no sense. But nothing in the world did right now.

The waiting continued. Intimidating. Interminable.

Intolerable.

Yet what choice did she have? She paced the

length of the room, played a game of gin rummy with Margaret, pushed away the thought of Gram's frail body being cut and spread and violated in the name of prolonging her life, when the treatment was equally as dangerous as the disease. She asked the nurses for updates. Was told the doctors had not "closed" yet. Be patient. Don't be alarmed.

Each time the door opened was cause for Kara's heart to stop. Each time the wrong person appeared she convinced herself that it was a good sign, not a reason to panic.

When Dr. Sloan finally did enter, one hand removing his surgical mask, she was so numb it took her brain a moment to register his presence. Then it ceased to function altogether until he smiled and said, "The surgery went well."

Her knees gave out. She collapsed into the chair from which she hadn't realized she'd risen.

Lisa and Major McKinney sandwiched her again, each holding one of her hands. They'd used a saphenous vein from Gram's right leg and an internal mammary artery from behind her collarbone. Triple—not double—bypass was needed, thus the longer amount of time in surgery. She would remain in recovery about two hours before moving to ICU.

She wasn't completely out of the woods, but Dr. Sloan was optimistic Gram would make a "satisfactory" recovery. Kara lost track of details after that. Maybe later more questions and doubts would arise.

But right now, "satisfactory" sounded extraordinarily excellent to Kara.

EIGHT HOURS LATER, Kara crept into her grandmother's ICU room with the same hushed reverence with which one might enter a majestic cathedral. State-of-the-art equipment hummed a Gregorian chant. Monitor screens glowed in stained-glass hues of green and blue. An antiseptic odor hung low to the floor, the medicinal incense stirring as she approached the narrow bed.

Gram's slight form lay shrouded in bandages. Plastic tubes nailed her to the altar of modern science. Her eyes were closed, her blue-gray curls mashed in disarray. Her mouth looked thin and colorless without its usual bright coat of lipstick. She looked so pale, so eerily still that Kara's gaze jerked to the steady blip to dispel her fear.

Her own pulse calming, she moved closer and stared down in silent gratitude and remorse. Gram would *hate* being seen like this if she were more alert. Visits were limited to ten minutes each hour per hospital rules. So far only Kara had come in. But Lisa, the Major and Travis were waiting their turn.

Travis had arrived an hour ago, his wild gaze bypassing the others to land on Kara. And what had she done? She'd walked straight into his open arms, that's what she'd done. Stupid and weak.

But, oh, how heavenly to feel his solid chest beneath her ear, hear his rumbling voice tell her Gram would be all right. She'd had to rip herself away before she clung and begged him not to let her go.

Blinking rapidly, Kara refocused on Gram. During an earlier visit, she'd drifted in and out of awareness, her eyes clouded with drugs and pain. Did she remember the letter? The shocking photograph of a granddaughter she'd raised to be a lady?

"I'm so sorry, Gram," Kara whispered brokenly.

Thin blue-veined eyelids fluttered once... twice...then opened to glittering slits. A fragile arm stirred in Kara's direction, and she sensed that her grandmother wanted to speak.

Her heart pounding, Kara lowered her ear next to an opening mouth.

"Don't leave me," a feeble parody of Gram's voice croaked.

Kara's eyes blurred. "No, I won't leave you, Gram. I promise. I'll take much better care of you from now on."

TWO DAYS LATER, in the formal living room of Taylor House, Kara shared the wine-red sofa with Suzanne Rogers, television critic for the *Houston Chronicle*. From matching wing-back chairs flanking the fireplace, Ross and Travis watched and listened intently. They'd already had their turn at being grilled.

A newspaper photographer sat on the love seat unloading film from a camera. He'd shot two rolls earlier during Kara's guided tour of the house.

Pencil poised above her notebook, Suzanne's demeanor was considerably warmer than when she'd begun the interview. "I'm sure our readers will appreciate your candor regarding what must have been difficult decisions for you to make. Thank you for allowing us a glimpse inside Taylor House."

Would this interview never end? "You're quite welcome."

Suzanne swept an admiring gaze around the room. "I can certainly see why your grandmother is determined to keep Taylor House in the family. It's lovely."

"Yes. We think so." Would the woman never shut that stupid notebook and leave? Gram would be waiting for Kara's visit.

"Is there anything else you'd like to add in closing, regarding your identity as the *Mystery Woman* model?"

Kara's mind raced. What had she already said? What had she not said? She glanced at Travis.

You're doing great, he told her silently. *Hang in there. You're almost home free.*

Turning back to the reporter, Kara spoke from her heart. "In your preview write-up of 'Hear He,

Hear She,' you referred to me as 'the voice of the new millennium woman.' That woman is strong, confident and independent. She's following blazed trails to the glass ceilings that stopped her sisters, then she's crashing through. She's also deciding to turn around half-way down the trail and head back to home and hearth, if that makes more sense for her. Or she combines the two as best she can. There's no right or wrong. Society finally approves of whatever role works best for today's woman. Except one.''

Scribbling madly, Suzanne glanced up in question. ''Which is?''

''The one that doesn't take care of the house, or the kids, or the boyfriend or husband or employees or boss. The one that's totally about *her*. That determines her sense of femininity and sexuality. It doesn't even have a name, it's so ignored by mainstream society.'' Kara groped for a word.

''Maybe 'lover'?'' Suzanne suggested, looking intrigued.

''No. That role involves someone else. There's a definite lack of respect and approval in mainstream America for anything that women do just for themselves. If you don't believe me, watch a man roll his eyes over his wife's hair appointment, but think nothing of paying big bucks for a round of golf. Listen to the sarcastic way people pronounce *Cosmopolitan* magazine. Or—this is one of the worst—

the way they snicker about 'those trashy romance novels.'"

The journalist smiled empathetically as she jotted shorthand.

Kara chose her next words carefully. "I guess what I'm trying to say is this—I don't think my involvement with the *Mystery Women* catalog is in conflict with my role as 'the voice of the new millennium woman.' In fact, I think it's the missing piece that was needed for me to represent the total woman, not simply the part society tolerates."

Finishing her notes with a flourish, Suzanne looked up with a broad smile. "Well! That's quite a wrap-up. And I have to admit I'm fascinated with your theory and inclined to agree with you. Thank you, all." She included Ross and Travis in her glance. "Between the three of you, I've got the makings for a hell of a rebuttal to the *Houston Express* 'scoop.'"

Her eyes gleaming competitively, she flipped shut the notebook at last.

Kara stood along with everyone else as goodbyes were said, wondering if she'd committed some huge publicity error by voicing thoughts she hadn't crystallized until today.

With a final wave at Suzanne and the photographer, Kara closed the front door and turned.

Ross let out a war whoop, scooped her into a

huge hug and spun her in a circle. She came down dizzy and breathless and laughing.

"You were brilliant!" he exulted. "She loved you! I love you! Marry me and have my children, but only blond green-eyed angels like you, okay?"

Her gaze snapped to dark eyes filled with memory and a possessive glitter.

Flushing, she broke the connection and shoved Ross's arm. "Nope. I only want little devils." *Brown-eyed and dark-haired, if you please.*

CHAPTER FIFTEEN

TRAVIS TROLLED the lot of Malloy Sporting Goods for an empty space, stunned at the huge number of parked cars for 11:00 a.m. on a Friday. The three days following Thanksgiving were always kind to retailers. But this year's annual "Gobble Up Savings" sale could very well break a store record.

Dad had budgeted more money for advertising than ever before. He must be thrilled. Travis sure as hell was. The TV commercial hadn't bombed.

What a relief!

Only three episodes of *Hear He, Hear She* had aired, though two more were "in the can." Travis had worried he couldn't deliver "celebrity clout" as a spokesperson for the store, even though the show had generated word-of-mouth buzz. Kara's leaked identity as the *Mystery Woman* had turned into a huge asset, launched by the feature article Suzanne Rogers had written. Local broadcast media had jumped on the bandwagon. Studio audience tickets were in hot demand. *People* magazine had even printed a blurb about The Relationship Channel and its dynamic new talk-show hosts.

Dynamic during taping. Afterward, Kara went straight to Taylor House. Esther's recovery had been steady. She'd pushed herself hard and was up to walking a half mile now, bless her stubborn heart. He was thrilled with her progress, but couldn't help wishing Kara was free to spend more time with him.

Parking on the outskirts of the lot, Travis decided he didn't really care why people were here, just that they were. And that they bought something, didn't merely browse. He locked the Jeep, walked to the main entrance, pushed through the glass doors—and pulled up short.

Jeez Louise.

Each car must've had passengers. Customers of all ages and sexes milled about, many craning their heads with unmistakable I-need-help frowns.

Not a good sign.

The ones he couldn't see were no doubt opening sealed packages to make sure the product looked like the photograph, reshelving rejected merchandise where it didn't belong, or any number of equally endearing things. He searched the store for his father and brother.

Dave, the only full-time employee besides Jake, manned the register next to camping equipment. Thomas, a part-time teenage employee, handled the one near apparel. Jake was in charge of the Customer Service counter. Lucky him.

All three had harried expressions and a line of impatient customers waiting their turn. Near a wall of display athletic shoes, his father carried a shoebox toward a mother and boy. No sign of Harry or Rick, the other part-time salesmen sometimes employed on weekends.

Expelling an aggrieved breath, Travis knew there was no help for it. Time to roll up his sleeves and pitch in.

He headed toward the shoe department, self-conscious as customers stared at his face without speaking, then commented behind his back.

"That's him!" a middle-aged woman whispered to her husband.

"He's so-o hot," a teenage girl told her giggling friend.

"Where's the blond babe?" a high-school jock asked his buddy.

"Nice ass," a woman in her twenties murmured to herself.

Travis's neck heated. *Nice ass?* Did these gawking strangers think he was deaf? If people were this rude to *him*, what kind of treatment was Kara getting?

A surge of ugly emotion followed the thought.

He could barely tolerate knowing men drooled over Kara as the *Mystery Woman* model. If he ever heard a male fan of the show mention *any* part of her anatomy with disrespect—

A hand grabbed his arm from behind.

He whirled around with fists raised.

The middle-aged woman he'd passed earlier stepped back with a frightened squeak.

Real smooth, Malloy. He lowered his arms sheepishly.

Her lanky husband moved beside her, laid one hand on her plump shoulder and extended the other for a brief man-to-man shake. "Warren Tate. This is my wife, Millie. She sneaks up behind me, all the time, too." His blue eyes twinkled. "Maybe if I took up boxing she'd break the habit."

"War-ren." Millie made a tittering noise.

Travis scratched his chin and smiled ruefully. "Sorry about that, Millie. I had my mind on something else. Can I help you with something?"

She tittered again and fingered the neck of her sweatshirt as if it were a strand of pearls. "I watch your show every week, Mr. Malloy—"

"Travis," he corrected.

She flushed with pleasure. "Travis. I think it's just wonderful how you and Kara help couples communicate better. I've told all my friends about the show, and now they wouldn't miss it for anything."

"Thank you, Millie. I'll be sure and pass the compliment on to Kara."

"*Would* you?" Ttt-tt-tt. "My friends and I think you two make the *cutest* couple. We just love the way you don't always agree, yet listen to each other with an open mind.'' She reached up and clasped the hand draped over her shoulder. ''We think that's so important in a relationship. Respecting each other, I mean. It's kept our marriage strong for thirty-one years, isn't that right, Warren?''

''Twenty-nine of the happiest years of my life,'' he agreed, deadpan.

''O-oh you,'' she scolded, bumping her substantial hip against his bony frame. ''Always kidding.''

Travis saw the quick squeeze of Warren's fingers, the loving affection on both faces, and suffered a sharp pang of envy. ''Well, it was nice meeting you both. Glad you enjoy the show, Millie.''

Warren spoke up. ''I'll hafta watch it next week and see what all the fuss is about.''

''Warren.'' Ttt-tt-tt. ''Don't mind him. He's such a kidder.''

Grinning his understanding, Travis saluted loosely and turned around, startled to see that people had moved in closer from all directions to stare at him.

Too weird.

Eyes straight ahead, he walked the rest of the way to the shoe department at a brisk pace.

John Malloy sat crouched in front of a boy around ten years old, his thumb pressing down on the toe of a high-top sneaker. He took his time, totally focused on the task.

"He's got plenty of growing room," he assured the kid's hovering mother. "Let's have him walk around and see how it feels."

As Travis approached the threesome, the woman's eyes met his and widened with recognition.

He placed a warning finger over his mouth, then assumed a querulous voice. "What'll it take to get some help around here, mister?"

John's head snapped up, the stark relief on his face at the sight of his son almost comical. Excusing himself to the boy's mother, he rose and waved Travis into the nearby stockroom.

The familiar smell of cardboard boxes, new leather and rubber soles brought back a thousand memories. Although he hadn't chosen to join the family business, he knew almost as much as his father about every phase of operation.

John turned and smiled. "Thank God you're here! When I couldn't reach Harry or Rick, I called the camp to see if you could bail me out. Nancy said you were on your way."

"Got caught a little flat-footed, did you?"

"No kidding! It's been like this since we opened the doors. I'm an idiot for not scheduling more help, but who knew we'd get this kind of response?"

"Oh, ye of little faith."

"Hey, I'm a believer now. But I'm slowly losing my flock. I've already seen several customers walk out mad when I couldn't get to them fast enough."

Since satisfied customers came before hunger, fatigue or a social life in the Malloy family, Travis knew what the admission cost his father.

"Where do you need me?" he said simply.

"On the floor. Preferably near the doors. Maybe you can prevent some of the walk-outs."

Nodding, Travis started to move, only to be stopped by the squeeze of strong fingers on his shoulder.

"I'm sorry about this, son. I know you don't have the time to spare. I'll make it up to you somehow."

"Don't insult yourself."

"Insult myself?"

Travis thought of the dark months after Kara left when his father had kept him and the camp going. "Who do you think taught me my priorities, Dad?"

As understanding dawned, John's dark eyes filled with immense love and deep humility. "There's something that's been on my mind that I've got to say, and I don't know when I'll get another chance."

The hand on his shoulder tensed, and Travis prepared for the worst.

"You've built a fine reputation as a top angler

and fishing guide. Lord knows I respect that. But in the past few weeks, I've watched you on the show and damn near popped my buttons with pride. You've matured, Travis. So much it's made me take a good hard look at myself. I'm not proud of the advice I gave you about keeping your distance from Kara.''

Surprised pleasure at his father's praise changed to wariness.

''You're a grown man and make your own decisions. But if I influenced you at all...well, I'd hate to see you spend the rest of your life with fish instead of a woman. If you love her—'' John squeezed his fingers ''—I mean love her body, mind and soul the way I did your mother, don't let anyone or anything keep you apart. Including fear.'' His mouth twisted. ''*Especially* fear.''

Inside Travis, something edgy and painful shifted, like a dislocated shoulder slipping back into socket. The look he exchanged with his father acknowledged emotions they'd protected and loneliness they'd experienced and hope for new beginnings—for them both.

''Okay, son?''

The lump in Travis's throat blocked the *O* in his answer, '''kay.''

They both laughed overly loudly, releasing emotion in an acceptable manner.

John clapped Travis on the back. ''We'd better

get out there before I lose more customers. Ready to face that crowd?''

Travis would've faced a lynch mob without hesitating. ''Piece of cake. Oh, by the way,'' he couldn't resist adding, ''Jeremy left this morning with Bobby Miller's family for San Antonio. Nancy will be by herself till Sunday.''

Leaving his father blinking at stacks of shoe boxes, he headed toward the front of the store, a new bounce in his step. The world was suddenly brighter, not because he'd gotten permission to love Kara. But because he'd quit denying to himself that he did.

He'd never *stopped* loving her, truth be told, although his feelings were different now from those of an eager young groom. Whether he felt the body, mind and soul kind of love his father had spoken of, or something less, Travis didn't know. Any more than he knew what Kara, the woman, felt for him.

Only one thing was as certain as the sun rising and setting.

He damn sure intended to find out.

CHAPTER SIXTEEN

KARA DROVE SLOWLY along the narrow road fronting five small shoreline houses. In the background, Lake Kimberly reflected the early-morning rays.

Sundays always drew hordes of pleasure seekers to the lake. On the Thanksgiving holiday weekend, with weather this gorgeous, the scattering of visible boats on the water would soon triple in number.

She refocused on the houses. Rats. Nancy didn't own a car, so Kara couldn't identify the cottage her friend rented by the vehicle in a driveway. She'd been so certain she would recognize George Weller's place—wait! Was that John Malloy's Blazer parked next to the fourth house up ahead?

As Kara slowed her Toyota to a crawl, the front door opened and John backed out onto the small porch. Nancy, dressed in a long terry robe, leaned against the doorjamb and smiled. He started to turn, obviously changed his mind and surged forward to haul her into his arms for a back-bending kiss.

Whoa, Mama!

Kara pressed on the gas pedal and sped away before they came up for air. If she'd been here ten minutes earlier, she might've knocked on the door at a very awkward moment. Thank goodness she'd stopped at Dunkin' Donuts first!

Despite her burning cheeks, she found herself grinning. Travis had told her Seth believed their father had the hots for Nancy. Kara had hoped it was true. And boy, was it ever! Good for Nancy. Good for them both, from the looks of that "Damn, but I wish I could stay" farewell kiss.

Kara's grin faded. The restless discontent that had plagued her since she'd awakened returned with a vengeance.

Okay, now what? The stop sign ahead intersected the blacktop road leading to the freeway. She braked, undecided, and sat with the engine idling.

Rolling down the window, she inhaled the tangy scent of fresh pine in air-conditioned outdoors. Glorious zero humidity. Not to be taken lightly by any Houstonian. But she really shouldn't play hooky.

She *should* turn left, drive back to Houston and log in some time at Taylor Fine Foundations. The store was temporarily closed until she had a chance to think straight. But her catalog orders were streaming in and taking up the slack. She had a ton of paperwork. And Gram needed…what? Not coddling, as she'd informed Kara sharply on Thanksgiving.

After she'd slaved half the day to cook a good— well, decent—okay, edible turkey with all the fixings, too. The way Gram had flirted with Major McKinney, Kara had felt like the odd man out. But in the hospital, *Gram* had been the one to plead with Kara not to leave. She'd been stunned, and filled with overwhelming devotion and, yes, pathetic gratitude. She'd never doubted her grandmother's love.

But in all Kara's thirty years, no one had ever seemed to sweat too much over whether she stayed or she left.

Ugh, ugh, ugh.

She was sick of worrying. She was sick of working. She was sick of expending energy and patience she didn't have, when her frayed nerves screamed for peace and solitude.

John would drive up behind her any minute if she didn't get moving.

She turned right.

Instantly her stomach churned. Sheesh. This is what she got for acting on impulse. After a night of fitful sleep, she'd tossed back her covers at dawn, tired but jittery, desperately needing a change of scenery and maybe some relaxed woman-to-woman coffee talk. Since Lisa wasn't human, much less companionable until noon, Kara had recalled Travis mentioning he'd given his assistant the weekend off.

So she'd showered, written a note to her grandmother and headed out for Lake Kimberly without phoning first. She'd wanted to let Nancy sleep as late as possible. Which, according to her, was never past eight since Jeremy woke with the birds.

Kara stiffened. Where had Jeremy been while his mother's toes were curling?

None of your business, Kara Ann Taylor.

Jerked into awareness of her surroundings, she realized she'd stopped in front of the Bass Busters Fishing Camp mailbox. The aluminum gate, normally closed, leaned open against a dam of earth it had bulldozed forward.

Her gaze moved from the entrance to the box of glazed donuts beside her on the passenger seat, back to the open gate. Why not? Travis was probably out fishing with clients, anyway. She reached for her purse and pulled out her compact mirror.

Fresh powder and lipstick couldn't disguise weariness from weeks of stress and poor sleep, but Kara did the best she could. Fluffing her hair, she watched the blond strands catch the light and paused. Comparing the color of her hair to a "leaping bass" wasn't the most flattering compliment she'd ever received, but an endearing one she still treasured. She refocused on the small mirror.

The woman staring back wore a tender dreamy expression.

Frowning, Kara snapped the compact shut and drove defiantly through the open gate. So her thoughts dwelled on Travis a lot these days. What of it? They spent a lot of time together, due to the show.

Good grief, it wasn't as if she'd washed her hair that morning specifically with Travis in mind, or driven straight to the fishing camp. If she'd planned on seeing him, she wouldn't have thrown on old faded jeans and dingy scuffed sneakers.

She'd worn her new mauve sweater made of clingy silk knit to cheer herself up. No other reason.

Just then the Toyota broke out of the woods and into the camp clearing. A welcome distraction. Braking, she stared at the horizon, newly struck by the spectacular view.

The vast blue lake sparkled and winked, tossing whitecaps coquettishly. Luring all who watched from afar to come closer, glide over her surface, explore her curvy shoreline, discover her mysterious depths.

Kara waited for a familiar rush of jealousy to erase her admiration.

Nothing. Not even a twinge of resentment.

In its absence, she found herself appreciating the camp as never before. Travis had been wise to keep things rustic. The undisturbed natural setting and sense of isolation were rare commodities so close to the city. Terrific "unique selling points." Basic marketing 101 principles. Yet, as Travis's wife, she'd lobbied long and hard to modernize the camp. Why? she wondered uneasily.

Kara didn't at all like the answer that popped in her head.

Had she subconsciously sabotaged the business that claimed her husband's time and attention—attention she'd wanted only on *her?* Shifting her foot to the gas pedal, she drove over the uneven road toward the house.

Of course she hadn't…had she?

Impatient with her doubt, she directed a sweeping glance over the grounds. Odd. There was Travis's Jeep next to the house, but no other cars were in sight. She would've thought most, if not all, of the cabins would be booked on this holiday weekend.

A movement on the pier caught her eye. The boat-shed door swung open. Travis stepped out and shaded his eyes with a palm.

Her breath hitched. A flock of starlings took off in her stomach.

Somehow she managed a reasonable job of parking next to the Jeep. She grabbed the box of donuts and slid out of the car, her gaze returning to the pier.

He walked at a near jog, alarm in every line of his body. Clearly he thought something was wrong. A natural assumption. She hadn't been back to the camp since the day she'd driven here with Ross. Now she'd shown up unannounced. Not to mention alone.

Moving to the top of the slope leading down to the lake, she clutched the box of donuts against her chest and waved reassuringly with her opposite hand.

Travis stopped midway between the boat shed and shore, then set his knuckles at his waist.

Her arm drifted down unnoticed.

Oh, what a glorious picture he made against water and sky! His stance wide, his shoulders wider, his dark hair lifting in the breeze. Wearing work boots, jeans with holes in the knees and a faded green sweatshirt, he reduced most other men she knew to sissies.

If testosterone was the only force at work, she could've ignored her reaction. But his formidable intelligence and wry humor, his responsible work ethic and basic kindness made the entire sexy package a Pandora's box of questions yet to be answered…to hell with consequences. Her feet began moving.

He might have tied a rope around her waist and hauled her in hand-over-hand, so compelling was the pull of his personality.

This was what she'd wanted upon awakening. To be with Travis. To see if the emotional bond she'd felt strengthening between them for weeks was as strong as the physical attraction that had always been powerful.

Slowly, helplessly, she walked down the grassy

slope and onto the pier. He stood unmoving, alert and watchful, while she approached and stopped an arm's length away. Tilting back her head, Kara searched his eyes.

Something pleased and very male gleamed there, giving her the disconcerting impression her arrival played into a goal she couldn't fathom.

"Good morning," she said, startled to hear the Mystery Woman's voice instead of her own.

His smile came slow and lazy, glinting white against the dark stubble he hadn't shaved. "'Morning."

"Don't worry. I'm not here because of a problem. Everything's fine."

"You got that right. You must've read my mind."

"How so?"

"Because I woke up and lay in bed thinking about you a long time. And the longer I thought—" his focus dropped to her mouth and lingered "—the hungrier I got."

Oh, my.

His gaze lowered deliberately to her chest. He gave a deep hum of satisfaction. "Are those for me?"

"Wh-what?" she squeaked.

He looked up with feigned innocence. "Those donuts. I figure you brought 'em here for a reason."

"Oh. Y-yes, of course." More flustered than she

could ever remember, she relaxed her hold on the box crushed against one breast. "Have as many as you want. They're glazed. I know you like the ones with sprinkles, but the man swore he just made these. They were warm when I bought them, so I think he was telling the truth. If they're stale, you can always pop them in the microwave. Not more than fifteen seconds, or they'll turn hard instead of soft—"

"Kara?"

She cursed her fair complexion. "Yes?"

"You're babbling, honey."

Could a tiger's eyes be feral *and* tender? "I know. I can't seem to help it."

"Then babble something I want to know. Like why you drove all the way out here from Houston. Not to bring me squashed donuts, I'm sure."

Kara glanced down, grimaced, and relaxed her death grip for the second time. "Sorry. They were originally for Nancy, but she had...company this morning."

"Company?" In a blink, the predatory gleam in his eyes vanished. "As in, male company?"

Seizing the chance to rattle *him,* Kara smirked. "Definitely male."

"Damn!" Thrusting one hand through his hair, Travis plunged the other into his pocket. "Whatever you do, don't tell Dad. I'll never get him to ask her out if he thinks she's seeing someone."

"Oh, she's seeing someone, all right. And from the looks of their goodbye kiss as I drove past, he did a lot more than ask her out last night."

Travis's dark brows rose, then slashed down. He scowled at his boots a long moment, looking so disgruntled and dejected Kara lost pleasure in teasing him.

"Travis, the man I saw kissing Nancy was your *father*."

His head shot up, his gaze piercing. "Seriously?"

She smiled. "Seriously."

The corners of his mouth lifted. He jingled his pocket change. "So...it was a hot kiss, huh?"

Kara fanned her face and laughed. "Oh, yeah."

Rocking back on his heels, he broke into a pleased chuckle. "Well whaddaya know?" *Jingle, jingle.* "You really think they did the deed?"

Picturing John sweep Nancy into his arms, Kara suffered an envious pang of yearning. "Absolutely."

Jingle, jingle. "How can you be so sure?"

The years dissolved. She was wrapped in her silk robe on the kitchen stoop, being hauled willingly into strong arms. "They were kissing the way we used to before one of your tournaments. Like she couldn't bear for him to leave. Like he wanted to drag her back inside and..." Kara trailed off, dismayed at where she'd steered his thoughts.

His features had grown taut, his body still.

The tiger was back.

"And what, Kara?"

She'd been stupid, stupid, stupid to mention the past, which always led to pain. She wanted to concentrate on the future. "It doesn't matter."

A gust of wind whipped her hair and buffeted her clothes. That's why she shivered. Not because his eyes said he remembered back-bending goodbye kisses, desperate and yearning, bittersweet with impending separation.

"It matters, Kara." His voice sounded as raspy as his beard looked. "When the sex is that damn good, it matters."

Sex, not love. The part of their relationship he'd missed the most after their divorce.

The only part he still misses, foolish woman.

His hand lifted and her pulse went berserk. But he only released a lock of hair sticking to her lips and tucked the strands behind one ear, then drew his index fingertip slowly and deliciously down her neck.

Kara shivered again.

"Cold?"

She followed the direction of his knowing gaze and flushed. Her thin knit sweater left little to his imagination. As usual, her body had responded to his touch, betraying her common sense.

"I've got to go," she muttered, backing away

slowly, desperate to put some space between them. She caught his startled glance an instant before she turned around and began walking.

"Kara?"

"I have to get back to Gram," she called over her shoulder, picking up her pace. "I'll see you on Tuesday."

"Don't do this, Kara." His voice rumbled deep, a warning growl.

She walked faster.

Purposeful bootsteps clomped on plank boards.

A thrill of fear, primitive and feminine, spurred her into a lope.

His bootsteps quickened. *"Kara!"* he roared.

Reason fled. Instinct took over.

She broke into a full run, her senses tuned toward the pounding behind her, and leaped from boards onto dead winter grass. The car. Get up the slope to the car. Faster! Don't look back!

Her worn sneaker soles slipped. She went down on one knee, scrambled up in a flash. Hurry! The hair on her neck lifted. She sensed his heat, his power, his concentration, his anger. Any second he would pounce.

Twisting, she shrieked and flung the mangled box of donuts into his astonished face.

It gained her maybe three seconds.

Big hands clasped her waist from behind. Her feet pedaled the slick grass. She toppled forward onto the slope, Travis holding much of her weight to break the fall. A gallantry he canceled by collapsing on top of her.

Hard.

The air exploded from her lungs. Kara suddenly knew how a whoopie cushion felt. She opened her mouth to laugh—and panicked.

Awful. Hideous. Not funny at all. She flailed weakly, unable to drag in a breath. The crushing pressure on her back eased. She was flipped over.

Her compressed lungs sucked in great gulps of sweet oxygen. The fog shrouding her brain cleared. Instead of sky, she saw Travis. Her awareness sharpened. Two facts registered.

He lay wedged between her legs.

And he was furious.

His stiff arms, bracketing her head and supporting his upraised torso, vibrated with tension. He glared down as if he'd like to squeeze the breath from her permanently.

"Are you crazy?"

Sometimes the best defense was offense. "Why, no, my ribs aren't broken. Thanks for your concern."

He appeared to be counting mentally for patience. Not a good sign.

"Let me up, please."

"No."

Stay calm. He has a right to be angry. "No?"

"Are you crazy *and* deaf? Jeez, Kara, why did you run away like that?"

Scowling, she cupped her ear. "Eh? What's that you said? Speak louder."

"Stop joking and answer me."

Her own temper flared. "Okay, think back. You were toying with my emotions from the first. That crack about the cold was the last straw. Since you can't seem to show me any respect, I decided not to stick around."

He looked genuinely outraged. "I respect you."

"Puh-leez."

His scowl deepened. "I do."

"Yeah? Maybe if I grew breasts on top of my head you'd look up to me, but a minute ago, you were being a jerk. So I walked away."

A fascinating dark stain spilled into his cheeks. "You *ran* away," he corrected. "And as long as we're talking about lack of respect, Miss Politically Correct, explain something to me, would you? Why do you *always* run away from me?" The sharp edge in his voice was closer to hurt than anger.

Rats almighty, she didn't want to get into this now. "I don't always run away. I've been rehearsing and taping shows with you for the past month."

"What about nine years ago?"

"Let me up, please. Gram's expecting me."

"Talk to me. Then I'll let you go."

She moved experimentally.

He lowered himself to his forearms, trapping her more effectively.

"I don't believe this," she said through her teeth. "Let. Me. Up."

"Talk. To. Me."

If she did, the fragile threads of her control would unravel. Real panic stirred. "I'll scream."

"Go ahead. I didn't book the cabins. There's no one around to hear."

She shoved at his immovable chest, bucked and squirmed to no avail. All she accomplished was to press herself against him more intimately. "Get off me, you elephant!"

"And let you run again? Dream on. I'm not budging until I get some answers. Why did you run away from me that night, Kara? Why did you *stay* away?"

"It won't change what happened. It doesn't matter."

"It was our *anniversary,* goddamn it! It *did* matter. *We* mattered."

Bone-deep pain and resentment seeped out of her marrow and into her bloodstream, the toxic emotions spreading insidiously fast.

She narrowed her eyes. "Where was all this righteous concern nine years ago, Travis?" The night she'd hoped to reconnect with a husband who'd become distant and disapproving.

"Oh, I had it, Kara. You just weren't there to see."

"I spent six hours shopping, cooking and primping for our big 'date.' You *promised* you'd be home by eight o'clock. You stood me up."

"I was late. There's a big difference."

Not big enough to prevent her naiveté from vanishing forever. "If you'd skipped the Yamaha tournament like I asked, we would've spent our anniversary together. It's fairly customary for newlyweds to think that's a special day."

"I placed second in the money, Kara. Enough to cover my tournament fees for the next year. I picked up my check and drove twelve hours to get home by eight o'clock."

"Gee, that's funny. I could've sworn that at *nine* o'clock I put all the food in the oven to rewarm."

"My radiator hose busted about ten miles north of Wharton."

She didn't want to hear this. It was too late to hear this.

"Pulling the boat and trailer was frying the engine. So I parked on the shoulder, raised the hood so people would know I had car trouble, then tried to hitch a ride into town." He huffed disgustedly. "Hell, everybody blew right past me. I probably looked like an escaped convict. I hadn't slept or eaten or shaved. I was royally pissed and wild to get home to you."

The image wrenched Kara's heart and filled her with dread. As the candles had slowly melted that night, so had her last dream of salvaging their marriage.

"After about forty-five minutes of cussing out taillights, I started walking. Took me almost two hours to get to Wharton and call you from Wal-Mart."

Kara jerked, and couldn't help noticing his body's instant reaction. Or her own response.

She ruthlessly ignored both. "You never called me."

"The *hell* I didn't."

"What time?"

"I dunno...nine-thirty? Give or take a few minutes."

"I didn't leave until after eleven. The phone never rang."

"I let the damn thing ring forever, Kara. Figured you were so mad you'd decided not to answer just to spite me. 'Course, I didn't realize I was grossly underestimating your capacity to hold a grudge..."

As his voice droned on, Kara's mind fast-forwarded through that fateful night.

She'd put the food away, opened the wine and proceeded to drink her fill of false bravado. Enough was enough, she'd decided. She'd tried to be the kind of wife Travis wanted. He sure hadn't worried about *her* needs. Commuting to Houston daily was too grueling for such a meager payoff. If he wanted their marriage to work, it was *his* turn to invest a little effort.

In the process of packing her things helter-skelter, she'd stumbled across a wrapped gift with her name on the tag. She'd wavered, then tossed it in her car, leaving the wrapped T-shirt she'd bought him—minus the sappy anniversary card—on an empty dinner plate at the table.

In all that time, no shrill ringing had interrupted her agony. And she hadn't left the house, except to pack the car and…

Kara groaned.

"What is it?" Travis asked sharply. "What's wrong?"

The filaments of her control stretched gossamer thin. "Mr. Parker."

"Huh?"

"Mr. Parker in Cabin Three. His toilet was running."

He paused. "Did you catch it?"

She choked out a miserable laugh. "Remember how the tank wouldn't fill sometimes? He came to the house and complained about the noise. So I went to his cabin and showed him the jiggle trick."

He absorbed the obvious. "At about nine-thirty?"

She nodded, and the first hot tear trickled free.

"That sucks."

The second tear meandered down her cheek. What was there to say about two destinies that had changed forever at the jiggle of a toilet handle? It was too laughably cruel, too painfully funny to contemplate.

Too simple an explanation, a rational inner voice cautioned. If she'd answered the phone, their marital problems wouldn't have vanished.

"So you left the house at eleven," he muttered. "By the time I bought a water hose, caught a ride to my truck and made the switch, it was close to ten-thirty. We must've missed each other by about forty-five minutes."

"Forty," she corrected, wiping a thumb beneath her eyes. "I was parked at Larry's Bait Shop when you drove past." She'd unwrapped his gift, the heart necklace, and known she couldn't leave until she learned he was safe.

"You *saw* me. And you didn't follow and let me explain?"

The betrayed accusation in his voice snapped Kara's control. "I was tired of doing the following! I needed to find out if you would follow *me*. If you thought a wife who oversalted egg salad and couldn't bait a hook was worth the effort to bring back. And I got my answer, didn't I, Travis?"

"Kara—"

"The next morning, I was calmer. Ready to listen to why you'd been late. But I wanted you to make the first move. That was vital.'' That was every-thing. It would've told her unequivocally that he loved her. ''When…you didn't come after me right away, I used to jump every time the phone rang, hoping it was you. My heart would pound when I sorted through the mail, looking for your letter. A card. Some indication you missed me at least a lit-tle. I would've come running if you'd crooked your finger. After six months without a word or sign, even I got the message you didn't *want* me to come back.''

He stroked a knuckle over her wet cheek. ''Kara—''

''No!'' She showed him her profile, sending a hot spill of liquid over the bridge of her nose. ''Let me finish.''

She hated his sympathy, hated feeling so ex-posed, hated herself most of all for turning the steering wheel right instead of left. But she was through running. She yanked her cowering ego out of hiding and thrust it into the light.

''When you rescued me at that fraternity party, I felt feminine and protected and petite for the first time in my life. I knew from the beginning I wasn't who you thought. But I let you believe I was like your mother. Like my grandmother. A domestic gracious lady. Your idea of the perfect wife.

''I let you marry an illusion, Travis, hoping you could learn to love the real me. But I hated housework and cooking, and wasn't the least bit gracious about doing domestic chores. I wasn't a good wife or helpmate to you. I wasn't mature enough to stay and work out our problems. The fact is, I wasn't..."

Rats, rats, rats.

Grass tickled one cheekbone; tears formed new tributaries over the other. She waited for the lump in her throat to shrink, then forced the words out. "I wasn't very lovable. I've told myself for years that you were to blame for our divorce. Another lie. If I'd been the woman you wanted, the woman you thought you'd married, our marriage wouldn't have failed."

For long seconds the galloping thud of her heartbeat filled her head to the exclusion of all else. Gradually, her awareness of other things returned.

The red ant crawling over a nearby blade of grass. The distant buzz of an outboard motor. The prickly sense of being watched and studied...

Oh no-o-o, Kara's mind wailed. Unlike petite women—who never swelled, reddened and/or splotched—she looked hideous after crying. The *coup de grâce* to her humiliation.

"Well," Travis said at last, propping his weight on one elbow. "That was quite a confession. Are you finished?"

Wishing desperately she could trade places with the mindless red ant, she gave a small nod.

"Good." He smoothed back the hair from her exposed sticky cheek. "Look at me, please."

And read the disgust in his eyes? Fat chance. "I did what you wanted and talked to you. Now you keep your promise and let me go."

Gentle fingers cupped her chin and forced her to face forward. She childishly squeezed her eyes shut, wringing out two fresh tears.

"Kara, Kara, Kara." His tsk-tsk was tender rather than mocking. "Haven't we learned that good communication allows equal time for both points of view?"

Eyes still closed, she nodded again.

"Okay. It's my turn to talk to you. So listen up." Squeezing her chin, he gave it a little shake. "I have a confession to make."

CHAPTER SEVENTEEN

A CONFESSION?

Behind closed lids, Kara pictured Travis's handsome face hovering close and wished she had the courage to peek at his expression. He'd surprised her again, intrigued her again, stirred faint hope again. She fought the irresistible tug of Pandora's box and waited for him to speak…

Well, rats. "Confess wh—"

She broke off as firm lips kissed one puffy eyelid, moved to the left and did the same, the pressure so soothing, so exquisitely tender she maneuvered her right lid under his mouth for repeat therapy.

When the warm compress traveled at random over her face, her mouth parted on a sigh.

"Kara, sweetheart," Travis crooned against her splotchy skin. "Why do you think I rushed you into marriage? You looked at me like I was a superhero. I had to land you fast—" he sipped a tear from her cheek "—before you learned the truth. Later, when you did, and I saw your disappointment, God help me—" he nibbled a path along the edge of her jaw

"—I couldn't face you. So I threw myself into building the business, told myself if I could make that work, you'd look at me like a superhero again."

Kara roused herself from dazed pleasure, her lids opening to slits. "The superhero always flies off and leaves the girl behind. I like mild-mannered reporters better."

Travis lifted his head. "*Now* you tell me."

Yes, a distant corner of her mind decided, a tiger's eyes *could* be tender as well as feral.

"Ah, Kara. We should've talked more. My fault. I accept the blame. You wanted marriage counseling, but I was too damn young, too full of wounded pride to admit failure. When you left me..." His face darkened into a brooding mask. "Something inside me died, I think. I lost a lot of weight—lost even more clients—and I didn't give a bass's ass. I didn't fish for at least six months. Maybe longer. That whole period is a little blurred for me."

Staggered by the admission, she could only stare.

"I was a fool not to beg you to come back, Kara. The problem with our marriage was *me*. Not you." His head swooped down, his expression savage.

A shower of quick fierce kisses rained upon her face, falling closer and ever closer to her breathless tingling mouth. Beneath the spangled drops of warmth, her nerves sizzled, her blood fired. Heat sluiced to every part of her that touched any part of him.

In a matter of seconds, she grew as hot and humid as a tropical rain forest.

Travis, Travis, she thought, her pulse a wild jungle drumbeat, *why did you tell me this? Why are you doing this?*

At that precise moment, the logical answer pressed for attention against her belly.

Stifling the urge to press back, she wrenched her head aside. His lips skittered to her temple and stopped.

He paused as if to collect himself, a thrilling notion. Plausible by the breath beating hard and fast on her brow, fanning her excitement, arousing desires only he had ever fully sated. She wanted nothing more than to raise the arms lying stiff at her sides and embrace what he offered. Mind-blowing passion, followed by...

Heart-shattering emptiness.

"What you do to me, Kara!" He turned and nuzzled her hair with a series of butting greedy motions. Like a kitten seeking a buried teat. "Mmm," he rumbled, more tiger than kitten. "You smell so good. Spicy and sweet...like you taste."

Her lashes drooped.

"When you left, I could still smell you. On the sheets. The towels. The afghan Esther knitted. On that silk robe with the little red flowers you forgot.

That was the worst—or the best? No, definitely the worst. It smelled *and* felt like your skin. Your robe made me crazy,'' he admitted with a seductive growl, his mouth lowering to her ear. ''I used to bury my nose in the thing and picture you wearing it, just so I could fantasize taking it off. And this morning, Kara? Lying in bed? For the first time in years, I let myself think of you naked in that robe. Then I tugged the sash loose and spread open the lapels, and damn near went insane itching to touch those beautiful breasts you don't want me looking at—''

''Don't,'' she pleaded, trying to roll her head away, realizing he'd trapped a mouse tail of hair beneath his big hand.

''Don't what? Don't fantasize? Don't look at your breasts? Don't want you so much I feel like my eyeballs are gonna bust?''

He drew back and thrust splayed fingers above her ears, sandwiching her skull, his gold-flecked eyes mesmerizing…burning…holding her captive more surely than his hands. ''Hundreds of men get off on *Mystery Woman* catalogs, imagining their hands all over your body, wondering what you look like under those scraps of lace. And you expect me to be immune? Hell, I look at your tight sweater and *know* that underneath, your skin feels like warm silk. I *know* that your breasts are the real McCoy and spill out of my palms.'' His voice grew strangled and strange. "I *know* they're tipped with cotton candy pink and taste like spun sugar and spice.

"Ask me not to breathe, Kara, and I might be able to manage it. But I can't look at you and not want you."

She burrowed her fingers into grass to keep them from dragging his head down for a kiss. "I'm not going to have sex with you, Travis, if that's what this is about."

He froze. His eyes narrowed. Slowly and deliberately, he slipped his hands from her hair.

So much for impassioned speeches.

"If sex is all I wanted from you, do you think I couldn't take it with your full cooperation? Don't kid yourself, Kara." Holding her gaze, he placed a palm on either side of her head, pushed up, and ground his hips forward in a circular motion.

Denim rasped against denim.

She moaned at the steamy friction, her pelvis tilting reflexively for fuller contact, her fingers rising involuntarily to clutch brawny shoulders, her throat arching spontaneously, vibrating with nine years of pent-up sexual yearning.

It was blissful.

It was pure torture.

She dug her nails into fleece-covered marble and whispered, "Stop."

Nostrils flared, eyes glittering, he ceased his merciless demonstration.

And her traitorous body ached and twinged and wept for more.

Fresh humiliation swept through her. "You've made your point. Now that we've clearly established I'm easy, would you *please* let me up?"

He looked incredulous. "Easy! You're the goddamn *hardest* woman to communicate with I've ever known."

Sliding down to settle less intimately between her thighs, he studied her with patent male exasperation. "I gut and fillet my soul, lay it right there on the table for you to wrap up and take home, or toss over with the rest of my carcass for the catfish to pick clean. And you assume I'm doing it just to get you in the sack?" He heaved a baffled sigh. "*I'm* not the one who doesn't respect you, Kara. Seems to me, you don't respect yourself."

Bingo.

His scowl vanished. Smoothing back her bangs, he peered at her closer, and paled. "Jeez, I'm right? You were *serious* earlier about being unlovable?"

I will not cry. I will not cry.

"Hell, I thought that was only I'm-gonna-go-eat-worms kind of talk."

No. She'd wanted to trade places with an ant.

Leaning down, he closed her stinging lids with his kiss, pulled away and anxiously searched her eyes. "What point do you think I've been trying to make? Listen carefully this time."

Once more he lowered his mouth, trailing his lips over her forehead, her cheek, the line of her jaw and back again. He used his lips like a skilled masseur, spreading words like a healing balm. "Everything about you is wonderful, Kara Ann Taylor. Wonderful and special and lovable. Your quick temper—" he kneaded away tension "—your quicker laugh—" he stimulated circulation "—your loyalty to Esther and family pride.

"Your bad cooking—" he massaged old wounds "—your good business sense—" he eased past aches "—the way your smile fills the hollow place inside me. I've missed you so much."

Her body glowed.

"I need you so much."

Her heart surged weightlessly in her chest.

"I love you so much."

Her soul burst joyfully free of burdensome doubt and fear.

"Please give us a second chance, Kara. I won't make the same mistakes. I'll give up tournaments. I'm damn sick of road trips and competition, anyway. I'll remodel the cabins and build a new boat shed, give the Marina a run for its money. You can drive into Houston every day like you did before, but I'll be waiting when you get home. I don't love a Suzy Homemaker illusion, I love you. To hell with housework. We'll hire a maid. I'll eat canned chili every night or stomach my own cooking. I haven't starved yet, but I think I'll die if I have to live without you again, Kara.''

Is this really me being ardently wooed by the man I love? The husband who let me pine a full year without uttering one word to bring me back?

"You need a web site for the catalogs," he continued, irresistibly earnest. "Net shopping is the wave of the future. Let me build you a *Mystery Woman* web site, like I did for the camp. I can help you build your business. Marry me, Kara, and I'll make you happy. I swear.''

Dizzy with wonder, she couldn't answer. Her eyes closed.

He pressed his cheek urgently to hers, wedged himself snugly where her blood had pooled. "Marry me, and I'll make you feel good, too. Don't deny that sex is important. It is. We were great together before. We'll be better now, I promise." His gruff voice took on a note of desperation. "What can I do to make you say yes?"

"Prove it." The answer slipped out before her conscious mind nodded approval.

"Okay, sure," he said eagerly, then paused. "Prove what?"

She smiled to herself, joy bubbling in her veins, and twined her arms around his neck. "Prove we'll be better than great together. Don't talk to me, Malloy. *Show* me.''

KARA STOOD in the kitchen amid glorious smells and congratulated herself on cooking her first perfect meal. Opening the old range oven they still hadn't replaced, she confirmed that the rack of lamb was golden brown and juicy, the surrounding roasted potatoes tender inside. Satisfied, she set the oven on warm.

Slamming the door shut with her hip, she stirred the pot of fresh green beans that were still firm and bright, glanced at the counter holding a triple-layer chocolate cake that leaned only a little. Travis wouldn't mind.

She wanted everything to be just right. To make up for everything that had been so wrong their first-year anniversary. If it killed her, their second first-year anniversary would be a date and memory they'd remember with joy. Not pain.

Kara checked the wall clock. Seven-fifteen. Travis would be home soon from Jeremy's class play. She'd wanted to go, too, but Nancy and John had known about her dinner ''date'' and insisted Jeremy would understand her absence.

More likely he wouldn't notice her absence, Kara thought affectionately. As long as his new stepfather and Travis were there, Jeremy would be in heaven. He adored them both.

Humming happily, she began setting the table exactly as it had been ten years ago, with tall tapered candles, a brightly wrapped gift on Travis's plate, a bud vase with one red rose. Had she forgotten anything? No. Yes! The wine.

She fetched the bottle of Bordeaux she'd bought in Houston last week after supervising the summer *Mystery Woman* catalog shoot. A good thing she'd gone. Steve was a talented photographer, but he had a tendency to create centerfold shots devoid of mystery and romance if left to his own devices. And Kara was adamant that the incognito model and lingerie seem feminine and sensual, rather than a man's idea of ''sexy.''

The model she selected each season was a new millennium woman—real in every sense of the word—from outside the fashion industry. Spring's catalog had featured a divorced mother raising two children alone on a waitress's salary and tips. Summer's would feature a graduate student financing her own way through law school. Both women had been extremely grateful to Kara for the anonymity and the generous modeling fee.

Setting the bottle and corkscrew beside the bud vase, Kara allowed herself a moment of professional pride. Mystery Woman, Inc. had recorded a two hundred percent increase in profits over the previous year. In the fall, she would introduce a line of Mystery Woman body lotions, bath oils, dusting powder and cologne to include with catalog and web site merchandise.

Taylor House was no longer threatened, though Taylor Fine Foundations was defunct. Gram had allowed the venerable store to die with dignity, rather than hang on past senility.

Giving the Bordeaux a last approving glance, Kara walked slowly toward the bedroom. After the shoot, she'd stopped by Taylor House for a wine recommendation. Major McKinney and Gram's wine-tasting class had made them four-week experts, doncha know. Now that he'd sold his home and moved in with Gram, they were always gadding about here or taking a class there. Kara chuckled.

Yep, her grandmother was living in sin, the tart. Major McKinney would marry Gram in a minute, if she weren't enjoying the risqué living arrangement so much. After a lifetime of conforming to rigid rules and Taylor standards, her brush with death had altered her priorities considerably.

Esther Taylor had become as close to a feminist as a feminine Southern belle had it in her to be.

Just then Kara passed the office. Unable to resist, she paused in the doorway to admire her new "stove." A sleek new Macintosh computer in eggplant purple for her very own. She cooked up all sorts of great desktop-publishing pieces for Bass Busters Fishing Camp on that baby. At least, she hoped they were great. Especially her most recent effort.

Rats. Now she was nervous.

Moving on, she headed for the bedroom's private bathroom, stripped off her clothes and stepped into the sparkling new shower stall. Travis had replaced the old one at the same time he'd redone the cabins' bathrooms. New pine paneling and king-size beds instead of the former bunks had completed the cabin renovations.

Expensive upgrades, but smart marketing, now that wives often joined their husbands on Lake Kimberly fishing trips.

Eight months ago Travis had guided a man and wife to more than some great fishing "points." He'd shared some communication tips with the couple. In turn, they'd referred two friends going through a rough marital patch to Travis's guide service. And so on, and so on.

Word had spread, and the camp now had one of the most unique selling points in the angler/guiding business. The camp's solitude and simplicity gave couples a chance to reconnect away from the frantic pace of modern urban life.

Kara switched off the water, towel dried and hurriedly dressed. She was applying fresh lipstick when the sound of tires crunching over the shell driveway grew loud, then stopped. The jungle drumbeat pounding low and steady in her blood for hours increased in tempo.

The front door rattled open and shut. "Lu-ceee, I'm ho-ome."

With an exhilarated laugh, Kara checked the bed-side alarm clock. Eight o'clock on the nose. Her heart swelled to bursting with love. "I'll be out in a minute. Why don't you pour us a glass of wine?"

"You got it."

Five minutes later she left the bedroom squeezed into the puckered stretch-velvet top and spandex skirt she'd first worn disco dancing, and then to a justice of the peace's office one year ago today. Not very practical, she admitted, tugging the tight material self-consciously. She felt less petite than ever before. But she hoped he would appreciate the sentimental gesture. Taking a deep breath, she entered the kitchen.

Travis had lit the candles, and stood pouring a second glass of wine. He looked up, and his eyes kindled with feral tenderness. *I missed you. I need you. I love you.*

"Watch out!" she warned, too late.

Wine dribbled over the rim, down the stem and onto the white tablecloth.

Grimacing, Travis set the bottle down. "Aw, hell, Kara. I'm sorry. The table looked so nice, too."

"It's not important." Like she could be irritated after the look he'd given her?

Kara walked forward and stopped close, thanking fate for putting them in the same *Vanessa Allen Show* audience. Thanking God for giving them the maturity not to try and change each other, but to accept and love who they were.

"Happy anniversary, husband. I've waited a long time to say that to you."

His eyes darkened. "Happy anniversary, wife. You look beautiful."

She looked down at herself ruefully. "Lisa would have a fit if she knew I was stretching out the Calendri original she so generously gave me."

A large warm hand came out to cover her slightly rounded belly, the move both protective and possessive. "Lisa will have a fit if you wait much longer to tell her you're pregnant. What are you waiting for?"

She'd told Travis she wanted to get past the first trimester before letting anyone know. But at four months and counting, it was past time to announce the news. "I know it sounds silly, but I didn't want to rub my happiness in her face. I kept thinking she might make an announcement of her own soon. It's so obvious they're in love! Even the fans can see it. Lauren told me they get tons of letters asking if Ross and Lisa are secretly married."

Travis slipped his arms around Kara in a comforting hug. "Give them time. They're learning with each show. They can't help it if they're not as sharp as we were." His chuckle rumbled against her ear, and she smiled.

After their eight-show commitment had been fulfilled, KLUV-TV management had pleaded with Kara and Travis to sign a new contract. At one point, Travis had snapped that Ross knew more about what was required than anyone—why didn't he co-host the damn show? Kara had jumped in saying Lisa would be the perfect foil, since they already debated every subject anyway.

The seed had been planted, and Ross had nurtured it to fruition. Now *Hear He, Hear She* was syndicated in sixteen major markets across the country.

Kara sighed. "You're right. Why don't we have everyone over for dinner next weekend and make the announcement? We can show them the finished cabins, too." Which reminded her...

"Sounds like a good plan to me," he agreed.

She gave him a fierce squeeze, stepped back and pulled him by the hand to his dinner plate. "Open your present."

"Now?" He blinked in surprise but picked up the slim rectangular box willingly. Shook it next to his ear. Grinned and predicted a tie.

"Open it!" Kara ordered.

He ripped off the gold bow and blue wrapping, opened the box and stared.

Rats, rats, rats. He hated it. "I can redesign the whole thing, no problem. I should've worked with you on it. I'm sorry."

Ignoring her, he lifted out a glossy four-color brochure featuring a front-panel photograph of the fishing camp and lake. Kara had wanted to feature the view as seen when one first broke out of the woods. Lisa had shot the panoramic view at sunset with stunning results.

Silently he unfolded the piece, looking at photos of the new cabins, several of him with clients holding up fish, one of a couple feeding catfish off the pier. He read the copy she'd lovingly slaved over to convey the essence of this special place. And when she saw his tanned throat work and was sure her gift had touched him immeasurably, her happiness knew no bounds.

He raised his shimmering eyes. "How?"

"Lisa took the photographs. I scanned them and did the design, layout and copy here at home. But I sent the file on disk to Vinnie. He piggybacked the job onto a *Mystery Woman* print run, so it cost practically nothing but the paper." Vinnie, who was crude but not stupid, had quickly forgiven Kara her deception when the potential of huge print jobs became apparent. "I hope you like it, because I've got a whole case of those suckers in the trunk of my car.''

''I love it. Almost as much as I love you.'' He leaned over and captured her mouth in a tender kiss. Breaking it far too soon, he pulled away and searched her eyes uneasily. ''I have something for you, too...but don't get excited. It's not jewelry, or anything like that. I didn't even wrap it—''

''Stop apologizing,'' she demanded, laughing. ''Whatever it is, I'll love it. Almost as much as I love you.''

Looking troubled, he reached back and pulled an envelope from his rear pocket. Something about his anxiety as he handed it over dried her throat and erased her smile.

Her heart pounding, she slipped out a folded note card and opened it to read a name and address.

Kenneth Mitchell
1467 West Lake Hill
Vancouver, Washington 98661

She looked at Travis blankly. ''I don't know this person.''

''I know, honey. And you don't ever have to, if that's the way you want it.''

Her heart hammered so hard she could barely breathe. ''Who is he?''

''Your father.'' He took one look at her face and gathered her close. ''Oh, Kara, I shouldn't have told you this way.''

Her father? He'd found her father? She pressed her cheek against his agitated heartbeat in dazed wonder.

"I knew how you felt about Jeremy's situation, and it broke my heart that you didn't have the option to talk to your father, if you wanted. So I hired a PI to track down Carol. He found her two months ago."

Kara's mind raced. Two months ago he'd driven to New Orleans with Jake to "keep him out of trouble" at the Louisiana Hunting and Fishing Exposition.

"She'd had time to regret the hornet's nest she stirred up, and gave him enough information to trace your father to Vancouver."

Kara knew there was much more to the story. But right now, the enormity of the news, and the love Travis had displayed in going to such lengths, overwhelmed any questions she had. Tears filled her eyes, riding the crest of irrepressible emotion.

She raised her head, clapped a hand behind his skull and pulled his mouth down to hers...

WRAPPED IN A silk robe, deliciously relaxed and ravenously hungry, Kara walked beside Travis into the kitchen. The candles had burned down to nubs. With a sinking stomach, she lifted the top to pale, mushy green beans, opened the oven door to dried, shriveled rack of lamb. Her perfect meal was ruined. She wanted to cry or throw a tantrum. Not exactly constructive communication.

She turned and eyed her husband narrowly. "Next year, Travis Dean Malloy, we're going *out* to dinner for our anniversary."

Coming soon from Jan Freed
and Harlequin Superromance, more stories
about the magnificent Malloy men! Be sure
to watch for them!

HARLEQUIN®
SUPERROMANCE®

By the Year 2000: BABY!

**What have *you* resolved to do by the year 2000?
These three women are having babies!**

Susan Kennedy's plan is to have a baby by the time she's forty—in
the year 2000. But the only man she can imagine as the father of her
child is her ex-husband, Michael!
MY BABIES AND ME by **Tara Taylor Quinn**
Available in October 1999

Nora Holloway is determined to adopt the baby who suddenly
appears in her life! And then the baby's uncle shows up....
DREAM BABY by **Ann Evans**
Available in November 1999

By the year 2000, the Irving Trust will end, unless Miranda has a
baby. She doesn't think there's much likelihood of that—until she
meets Joseph Wallace.
THE BABY TRUST by **Bobby Hutchinson**
Available in December 1999

Available at your favorite retail outlet.

HARLEQUIN®
Makes any time special ™

Visit us at www.romance.net   HSR2000B

Looking For More Romance?

Visit Romance.net

Look us up on-line at: http://www.romance.net

Check in daily for these and other exciting features:

Hot off the press

View all current titles, and purchase them on-line.

What do the stars have in store for you?

Horoscope

Hot deals

Exclusive offers available only at Romance.net

Plus, don't miss our interactive quizzes, contests and bonus gifts.

PWEB